Manuel
and the
Madman

# OTHER BOOKS BY GERALD W. HASLAM

## Fiction

Okies: Selected Stories
Masks: A Novel
The Wages of Sin: Collected Stories
Hawk Flights: Visions of the West
Snapshots: Glimpses of the Other California
The Man Who Cultivated Fire and Other Stories
That Constant Coyote: California Stories
Many Californias: Literature from the Golden State (editor)
Condor Dreams & Other Fictions
The Great Tejon Club Jubilee

## Nonfiction

Forgotten Pages of American Literature (editor)
The Language of the Oil Fields
Western Writing (editor)
California Heartland: Writing from the Great Central Valley
  (co-editor)
A Literary History of the American West (co-editor)
Voices of a Place: Social and Literary Essays from the Other
  California
Coming of Age in California: Personal Essays
The Other California: The Great Central Valley in Life and
  Letters
The Great Central Valley: California's Heartland
Workin' Man Blues: Country Music in California
Many Californias
Jack London's Golden State

# Manuel and the Madman

by
Gerald W. Haslam
Janice E. Haslam

Devil Mountain Books
P.O. Box 4115
Walnut Creek, CA 94596

Gerald W. Haslam & Janice E. Haslam

# Manuel and the Madman

Text Design: Janice E. Haslam
Cover Design: Garth Haslam
Cover illustration: Martha Molinaro & Garth Haslam
Special consultant: Clark Sturges
Copy editor: Alexandra Russell

---

Library of congress Cataloging-in-publication Data

Haslam, Gerald W.
    Manuel and the Madman / Gerald W. Haslam, Janice E.
      Haslam.
      p. cm

    ISBN: 0-915685-11-6
    1. Mexican Americans --Juvenile fiction. [ 1. Mexican
      Americans--Fiction. 2. Racially mixed people--Fiction.]
      I. Haslam, Janice E., 1940 - II . Title.
    PZ7.H27647 Man 2000
    [Fic]--dc21

---

For Choosie, Tigre, Flaco, Gola, Cheetah, Chava, Gordo, Mad Dog, Anton', Fuzzy, BeeJaw, Raymie, Duke, the Chief, *y los otros* — Bakersfield's best... and for Gary and Carolyn Soto, Fresno's finest.

# Manuel and the Madman

Ryan, Manuel
English 7A
Mr. Mancuso

*See me! Mr. M—*

"My Most Memorable Experience"

One time when I was just a little kid visiting my grandma, my friends Flaco and Keeny and *I* me were playing in my grandmas yard. Flaco said lets have a "F.P." contest. We were just little and we did not know any better, so we pulled are pants down. Little kid pants without zippers or anything, and we tried to "P." the furthest. But my grandmas' rooster that she called Taco he came around the corner and he pecked Keeny you know where.

Keeny he screamed real loud and took off for home without pulling his pants up or anythng and, his big brother Trini and, these other two high school guys they heard him and ran to see what happened. Keeny told them and they laughed real loud and, Keeny cried louder. Then his mother came out and she got real mad.

Who did this to you she hollored and, Keeny said it was Flacos' idea and, then Flaco told a big lie and said that I told him to do it and, then she said your in big trouble and, we both got spankings right on the street in front of every one.

In conclusion, that is when I should of quit liking Flaco.

## Chapter 1
# The Bike

Me and Flaco and Keeny we rode our bikes to the school that afternoon to mess around. I was on Keeny's rickety old one, while him and Flaco took turns on the new bicycle my dad had bought me. "Hey, Ryan, how come you're wearin' your cap that way?" Flaco called.

"That way?" I asked.

"Backwards, *ese\**, backwards?"

"Backwards?"

"You gots the bill in front, man."

"So? What's so big about it?"

"Hey, Keeny, look at Manuel's cap. He gots it on backwards," giggled Flaco.

Keeny glanced at me, and he laughed too. That made me mad, but these two guys were the only ones I really knew in this neighborhood, and I didn't want them to stop hanging out with me, so I turned my cap around. Big deal.

"Now you look cool, ese. Right, Keeny?"

"Simón, cabrón," he replied, his favorite expression.

When were pedaling past this pool hall named the

---

* A Spanish-English glossary may be found on pages 201-206

1

Eight-Ball, I noticed a decorated thing, almost like a monument or something, on the vacant lot next door. There was a bunch of mean-looking big guys wearing plaid shirts and headbands sitting on these old couches there too. One of them hollered, "Hey gringo, what're you doin' in this barrio? Go back where you belong before somebody kicks your little white ass." I heard the other big guys laugh.

I kept pumping fast until we were a block or two away, and I asked, "Was that big guy hollering at me?"

"Sure," said Flaco.

"How come?"

"You're not a homey, ese."

"I been coming here since I was little," I pointed out. "I was playin' with you guys since we were real little."

Even if I was scared of those big guys, I was curious about that other deal I'd seen on the lot: a big cross with some heart-shaped thing hanging on it, and a picture of somebody in the middle; there was writing on it, too, but I couldn't read anything because I was riding too fast when we went by. But I did glimpse plastic-looking flowers around, and one of those jars with an Our-Lady-of-Guadalupe candle burning in it. It looked weird. I asked, "What was that shrine thing back there?"

"That's where Joey Castro's brother got wasted, ese. Right there! You could see blood spots on the lot for a long time."

I'd visited my grandma's neighborhood ever since I was a baby, but I'd only been living here a month. I wasn't sure which stories about it to believe. "What do you mean, 'wasted'?"

"Some guys from the La Loma gang they shot him, ese," explained Keeny.

"They shot him. How come?"

"He looked at 'em. And he was wearin' the wrong colors, red."

"He looked at 'em? Wrong colors? That's dumb." I didn't believe him. They'd been telling me a lot of baloney stories since I'd moved in with my abuelita. Shooting and stuff like that was from the movies, not real life. "What's that about red?"

"Hey, we're Norteños, ese. Red's our color. Those cholos from La Loma , they're Sureños, blue's their color."

I didn't get it. "What's so big about colors? And what's that Sureño and Norteño stuff?"

"Hey," frowned Flaco, "me and Keeny're Norteños, ese...," he puffed up a little bit. "That means we're real Chicanos. You better watch what you say, Riley. The guys in the gang might shoot a gringo like you if you dis' 'em. Huh, Keeny."

"Simón, cabrón."

"Exspecially a gringo," Flaco added. "But they don't mess with me, ese."

He was the littlest guy in our class, so maybe he was too small a target. He had the biggest mouth, though. "What's dis' 'em mean, anyways?" I didn't know what they were talking about sometimes.

"Don't you know nothin', Manuel. If you don't give 'em their respec', ese."

This was all mumbo-jumbo to me. "Yeah," I said, "well it's still dumb. How come that guy called me a gringo, anyways?"

"You are a gringo, Ryan."

"I'm not any gringo," I told him.

"Don't you got a mirror? You got those freckles. You got that yellow hair. You're white, ese," Flaco asserted.

"Am not."

"Okay then," interrupted Keeny, "what are you, then."

That stopped me for a moment. "Me, a Mexican, I guess. Or Irish. Or something."

Keeny grinned. "Hey, Flaco's Irish, ese. He's smoked Irish!"

3

"You are, pendejo!" snapped Flaco. Then he said to me, "Besides, you're an American, ese."

"So? You guys're Americans too," I pointed out.

Flaco shook his head. "Not us, ese. Me and Keeny're Mexicans. Norteños."

"Bogus," I said. "How come you're not in Mexico then? You guys told me you were born in Bakersfield just like me. How come you're Mexicans then?"

That stopped Flaco for a second, then he said, "White guys're Americans. Brown guys're Mexicans, that's why, right Keeny?"

"Simón, cabrón."

After a second, I asked, "Then how come Raúl Ortega's a Mexican? He's white as me, and he's even got red hair."

That stumped them, so after pausing Flaco changed the subject. "No lie," he said, "those La Loma guys they really shot Castro's brother."

"What's La Loma, anyways?" I asked.

"Hey, Ryan, you don't know nothin'," Flaco grinned. "That's the name of another barrio over in East Bakersfield where all these Sureño cholos live. They're all dumb."

Sometimes I thought him and Keeny were dumb. It was like they lived in a different world than me. Anyways, after we got to the school we found some other guys from our class, and we played booty-on-the-board for a long time. That day the other guys didn't talk about me in Spanish too much. They teased me just a little bit because I was so pale, but no real mean stuff. They were getting used to me, I think. Besides, I was faster than any of them, so they always chose me for their teams.

When we got ready to go home, though, my new bike was gone. We looked everywhere, but it was really gone, like it disappeared. Great, I thought, welcome to Our Lady of Guadalupe School. That bike was the last thing my dad gave me before he left. Now I'd lost him and it both.

➤

4

## Chapter 2
# What Am I?

I know it's a bad sin, but sometimes I hate my dad. My mom too. Or I ought to, at least, because they moved away and left me here with my grandma. Mostly, though, I just want them to come back so we can be the same as before.

I don't see why I have to live with Abuelita, anyways. I don't hate her or anything, but I don't understand her a lot of the time. At least she hasn't left me...not yet anyways. And she hasn't told anybody that I started wetting the bed after Mama and Daddy went away. I try real hard not to, but I just wake up soaked some mornings. And she doesn't tell anybody that I've still got this little tiny piece of my baby blanket that I like to hold when I'm sad. It seems like I'm just sad a lot now that my folks're gone.

Abuelita really tries to help me with stuff, too, but sometimes I think she doesn't understand me any better than I do her. Like when I brought that form home from school.

"The teacher said we gotta fill this thing out, Abuelita," I said.

I unfolded the paper and placed it on the kitchen table

in front of her. She wrinkled her nose like a pale prune, then she examined the sheet, poked it with one of her fingers, and asked, "What *is* this thing, mi'jito?" Abuelita always acted that way about official-looking papers, like they were poison or something.

"It's just this form all us kids have to fill out. See what it says right there?" I pointed to the paragraph at the top of the page.

She squinted, then said, "Read it to your grandmother, mi'jito. My eyes are tired." She didn't believe in doctors, so she owned only a pair of glasses purchased at the drug store. They didn't work real good, and mostly I read to her.

I picked up the paper, shook it, then read: "Please indicate your race or ethnicity by placing a check in the proper box. Parents or guardians must sign for all minors. Completion of this survey is mandatory."

"...is mandatory?" she asked.

"That means we gotta do it."

"Oh," she shook her head, "the nuns say we must do it. Well, read to me what it says, mi'jito."

"It says, 'White/European, Native American, Asian, Black/African, Middle-Eastern, Pacific Islander, Mexican/ Chicano, Other Hispanic.' That's the list. What am I?"

She paused, then said, "Like me, you are Spanish."

"But my name's Manuel Ryan. Daddy's family was mostly Irish, and other stuff. How can I be Spanish?"

Her whole face pruned again like she'd just smelled the chicken coop. "That Irish," she spit. "He left you. Now you are Spanish like me."

That made me mad. "He never left me. He just had to go away to find a job. Besides, Mama told me I'm half-Mexican and half-American and that both mean we're mixtures of stuff, anyways."

Suddenly, Abuelita's face froze like a statue's, wrinkles

6

and all. She said very slowly, "We are Spanish. ¡Míre! Look at this skin." She stuck the pale underside of one of her arms under my nose. "Look at those blue veins," she ordered. "Spanish!" she said, nodding her head. "Your mother made a mistake. We are not Mexicans, we are Spanish. I will talk to her."

Boy, that stuff really got her mad. She was always talking about nationalities: she said the garbage man was a Portugee; this guy Nacho Cervántez's mother she was a Gypsie; the man who ran the little grocery was an Oriental; my pal Flaco's grandfather he was an Indio.

And she could tell you how they'd act because of what they were, too. "Those Irish all drink, you know," she said one day, not naming my father but raising her eyebrows real high like she was going to comb her hair with them — an I-told-you-so look.

Another time it was, "That Banducci boy in your class, Eye-talian. All dull-witted, you know."

"Eye-talian?" I said. Bobby Banducci was from Bakersfield like me. He didn't even understand Italian, and he was a straight-A student. I wished I was as smart as him.

And after my mom had urged Abuelita to see a physician, she said, "That doctor your mother wants me to see, a Jew! All they care about is money."

I'd just shrugged. Doctor Ostroff was cool, I thought.

Besides, I didn't see what was so big about it. And now I was supposed to be Spanish, but my mom had always told me she was Mexican and Daddy was mostly Irish.

Well, it never did any good to argue with my grandmother, so I just said, "Okay. Then which one am I?"

"Read to me that list again," she said, sounding calmer.

I read it once more, and she hesitated. Finally, she said, "Spanish."

"It doesn't got Spanish, Grandma."

Another pause, then she said, "What was that one after 'Mexican?'" She said that word funny, like it choked her.

"'Other Hispanic.'"

"Hispanic?"

"Yeah, 'Other Hispanic.'"

She smiled. "We are 'Hispanic' without the 'Other.' We are the *real* ones."

"Okay," I replied, and I slowly crossed off "Other," then placed a check in the box behind the remaining word. "All done," I said. "Sign it, okay."

"We are Spanish in this house," my grandmother added as she slowly wrote her name.

"Okay," I said, but I thought *big deal*.

Just then two high-pitched voices howled from the yard, "Maaaaan-nuel! Hey, Maaaaan-nuel!"

Flaco and Keeny were outside. They never ever knocked on the door when they could get away with yelling.

"Can I go out and play with the guys, Abuelita?"

"You have finished your homework?"

"Yeah."

"All right, my son." Then she added, "Those two malcriados, they are Mexicans, not Spanish like us."

Big deal, I thought again. "Okay," I said, then I sprinted out the door.

## Chapter 3
# "A Dirty Story"

"Hey, did you find your bike, ese?" asked Flaco.

"Naw," I shook my head. The policeman who'd come to investigate after we called, he said I'd probably never see it again. That made me real sad, not just because of the bike but because of my dad. These guys didn't know that I'd been sleeping with my blanket again ever since that lousy day somebody stole my bike, and I was having these sad dreams.

"If any dude ever takes my wheels, ese, I'll punch his lights out," bragged Flaco. "I'll sic Rollo on him." Rollo, his dog, was about as dangerous as him, real little, with this stiff hair all over. It bounced around and growled at everybody. Flaco, he said Rolo killed a pit bull one time, but his dog would only be able to bite a big dog's knee it was so little. It made a lot of noise, though ... just like its owner.

"Sure you would," I said. He was always *going* to beat somebody up.

"Hey, you wanna play cowboys with me and Keeny, ese?" he asked. "We can hide out in Mr. Samuelian's yard. Keeny can be the bad guy."

"You can be the bad guy, ese," Keeny snapped. "I'm

9

not being any bad guy. You can be one of those Mexican bad guys with the big sombreros and bullet belts across their chests."

"No way, pendejo."

Just then our next-door neighbor, Mr. Samuelian, wandered out into his yard. He noticed us and waved. We all waved back. He was a little guy, Mr. Samuelian, not much bigger than me, and about as old as my abuelita. He had this bushy sliver hair like that fluffy white stuff you can buy at Christmas, and big, white eyebrows too. He also had this great big, old-time mustache like the ones you see in pictures in history books. He was real fun, not like most grown-ups.

"You *are* a Mexican, pendejo," hissed Keeny, quietly so our neighbor wouldn't hear.

"And you're a pendejo, Mexican! I'm gonna be Clint Eastwood," Flaco insisted.

"You don't look like Clint Eastwood. Manuel looks like Clint Eastwood."

That stumped Flaco, so as usual he changed the subject: "If you make a face and think about bad stuff like a girl's boobs or something at the same time, your face'll stick that way. You have to make the sign of the Cross right away or it'll never change back."

"Beans," I said, "that's little-kid stuff."

"That guy Tony Blanco's father, that's what happened to him, ese. Huh, Keeny?"

"Simón, cabrón," nodded Keeny.

Half of Mr. Blanco's face slid down like melted wax, but the other half looked okay. "How do you know?" I demanded.

"You can tell just by looking. Huh, Keeny?"

"Simón, cabrón."

To me, it was too dumb to even talk about, so I suggested, "Let's go mess around next door. I'll bet Mr.

Samuelian'll let us. We can ask him about Mr. Blanco's face."

A shrill voice echoed down the block "Flaaaaaco! Flaaaaaco! My mother wants you!"

We knew whose little sister was calling him. She sounded like a siren. "Hey, how come she always says her mother wants you?" I asked Flaco. "Isn't she your mother too?"

"Because she's a dumb girl," he said. "See you guys," and he trotted down the street.

"What do you wanna do, ese?" Keeny asked. He sat on the broken-down couch that plopped like a retired hippopotamus in front of Abuelita's small house. The couch stunk in winter when it got wet, and it bulged in different places, but I liked it. It was great to wrestle on. Keeny had a seat from a car in his yard, but it wasn't as cool as the couch. My mom told me a long time ago that my grandpa, who died when I was little, he used to sit on the couch every day and talk with his friends. I couldn't remember him very good. Anyways, the couch had always been there.

Me and Keeny flopped on it for a minute, my grandma's little flock of chickens scratching and pecking around our feet, then he sort of looked around to make sure nobody else could hear, and asked, "Wanna hear a dirty story, ese?"

"Sure!"

"This little boy, he used to bring his teacher raisins to school every day, see. One day he never brought her some, and so she asked him why. He said, 'I would have, but my rabbit died.'" Keeny burst into laughter. "Get it, ese?" he said.

That was a dumb joke to me, so I said, "Is that the best one you know? Let's shoot baskets."

He wasn't real good at basketball, so he made a face when I suggested that, and asked, "Did you ever hear the one about the farmer's daughter and the traveling salesman?"

"Everybody's heard that one. Besides, your face's gonna a stick now because you were thinking of a dirty joke."

"Nah-uh," Keeny said, hurriedly crossing himself. "Let's go knock on doors and run away. We can watch people get mad."

"Don't make a face while you say that," I warned him.

"You're no fun," said Keeny, crossing himself again. "Besides, me and Flaco did it last night over by the school. This one guy, he had a doorbell and we rang it and ran three times and he hollered he was gonna call the cops, so we came home."

"That doesn't sound like much fun to me. Let's shoot hoops." I had the top of an old waste basket nailed to a tree, and had an old ball, not quite round, our neighbor Mr. Samuelian had given me. The ball didn't bounce real good, but at least you could shoot it. Me and Keeny played a game of H-O-R-S-E, then a game of twenty-one. I won both, so Keeny said, "This isn't any fun."

We were about to start another game of H-O-R-S-E, when Mrs. Alcalá, our next door neighbor and Keeny's great-aunt, she hobbled out of her house on her two canes, followed by her big tomcat, Tuxedo. She called, "Joaquin, your mother wants you home for dinner now. She telephoned me."

"Okay tía," he called.

He really didn't want to play another game, I bet.

"See you, Ryan," he said, and he took off.

"Is that you, Esperanza?" I heard my grandmother call to Mrs. Alcalá, and she walked over to talk to our neighbor.

## Chapter 4
# Neighbors

"Now that mad Armenian is cultivating fire," Grandma warned Mrs. Alcalá, nodding toward Mr. Samuelian's yard on the other side of ours. "He is a menace. Muy peligroso," she nodded, "a very dangerous man."

Mrs. Alcalá, as old as Abuelita remained unconvinced. "Ah, Lupe," she smiled, "you carry on about nothing. He harms no one."

"He harms me," my abuela insisted. "He is loco. He walks around that terrible, overgrown yard of his talking to himself. And singing sometimes. A grown man!"

"No, no," Mrs. Alcalá disagreed pleasantly across the drooping, unpainted fence that separated her small lot from ours. "The man is a poet. He simply recites his poems as he works in his yard. He is a good man, I tell you. Doesn't he give us all fruit?"

"I would never eat it," snapped Grandma. "Poisoned, you know."

That's what I mean about not understanding her. And she did things that my folks never had, like light candles for everything. When I told her my bike had been stolen, she pulled another candle from under the sink and placed it on the shelf above the TV, then lit it. "This sacred candela is for San Antonio," she explained. "He will find for you that bicycle." She had enough candles burning there to roast a horse, and uncle Tuti he'd put this shield deal there so she wouldn't burn the house down.

But Abuelita was usually nice, but she had some funny ideas too, and she'd get mad over silly stuff, and stay mad. My mom told me that Grandma didn't talk to one of her sisters for almost twenty years because they had an argument over a hat. Twenty whole years, almost twice as long as I've been alive. That seemed real dumb to me.

Anyways, after hearing about the poison, Mrs. Alcalá just chuckled. "Nonsense, I have eaten it for years."

Abuelita only snorted. She had often commented on our neighbor's poor health. "All right, Esperanza," she finally responded, "all right, but that madman is also growing fire in his yard, and when our neighborhood has been consumed and we are all burned to chicharrones, out on the street with no houses, then you will agree with me. Everyone will. But it will be too late!" Abuelita's voice was rising and her head was bobbing as she spoke. Spit was flying from her mouth and it kind of scared me. "One day those weeds of his will burst into flames! Mark my words!"

"Ah, Lupe," smiled our neighbor, "you must control yourself. Calm down. You're not a girl anymore. Besides, Mr. Samuelian grows plants, not fire. He is an unusual man, true, but not a bad one. He simply loves those plants of his. He waters them and they grow huge and green. Calm yourself, my friend, or you'll burst a blood vessel."

Abuelita seemed as agitated at Mrs. Alcalá as she was at the man she always referred to as the madman. "They are weeds! He is a menace!" she repeated.

Mrs. Alcalá merely smiled and shook her head.

Nearly everyone in our family agreed that my grandmother was a saint — she attended Mass regularly and never failed to receive Holy Communion. She was not, however, very popular among those who lived near her. Abuelita took pride in being what she called "plain spoken." Once, before my father moved away, I heard Mama describe Abuelita as "a woman who calls a spade a spade." Daddy said, "Yeah, and she calls a lot of other things spades too."

Mrs. Alcalá was the neighbor most tolerant of my grandmother. Mr. Samuelian also tried to be friendly, but my grandma would have nothing to do with him.

Abuelita's grudge against him had started the day he moved into the neighborhood, Keeny told me. He'd heard it from Mrs. Alcalá. He said my grandma'd asked Mr. Samuelian if he wasn't an Armenian. He'd said no, his parents had been Armenians but he was an American, born and raised in Fresno.

That answer had not pleased Abuelita, because she loved to assign people to her version of nationalities.

Mr. Samuelian had then asked what she was, and Abuelita had said, "Spanish."

"Spanish," he'd said. "What part of Spain are you from?"

Abuelita really didn't like that, since she had been born right here in Bakersfield, California like me. And Mama'd told me that my great-grandparents had come from Mexico, not Spain.

That was all it took I guess. "Voy a pagarlo en la misma moneda," Abuelita once said to me about Mr. Samuelian, and I didn't understand exactly, something about paying him in the same money. My Spanish wasn't too good because Daddy hadn't encouraged my mother to use that language much around me. He was afraid it might hurt me at school.

"You know how those Armenians are," Grandma hissed across the fence to Mrs. Alcalá that afternoon.

"No," replied our neighbor, "I don't. But Mr. Samuelian is friendly and smart." She held the vast, black-and-white Tuxedo. He was missing most of an ear due to one of his many battles, and had a milky eye thanks to my grandma's rooster Taco, but in our neighbor's embrace, he slit his eyes and purred, and hung there like a furry snake.

Abuelita appeared not to hear Mrs. Alcalá. "This used to be such a nice neighborhood, but now los otros are moving in."

Our neighbor sounded disgusted "No, Lupe, they are not the others, they are our new neighbors. Which of them are not friendly? You need to open your eyes." She turned, put Tuxedo down, then hobbled away on her two canes, shaking her head as she went.

"*I* need to!" exclaimed my grandmother. "*I* need to! A mad Armenian is growing fire and *I* need to!" her nostrils were puffing out. "A singing madman is cultivating weeds, and Esperanza Alcalá speaks to me as though I am a child," she was sputtering.

I wanted to hide my eyes because I hated to see her like that.

"One of these days I'm going to tell off Esperanza Alcalá, you can be certain of that!"

"Yes, Abuelita," I said. She was always going to tell someone off, usually Mrs. Alcalá.

Just then her eyes looked funny, then she grabbed the fence and braced herself.

"Are you okay, Abuelita?"

"Only a little dizzy spell, mi'jito," she said. "I am fine."

As we stood there, Flaco jogged by calling, "Rollo! Rollo!" He noticed me and said, "My dog he got out and I gotta catch him before he hurts somebody's dog," then he disappeared around the corner.

➤

## Chapter 5
# Mama and Daddy

After she got her balance back, my grandma still had this funny, sort of dazed look in her eyes, but she commented, "Too bad. I wonder sometimes if Esperanza's mind isn't slipping. Qué lástima. She cannot see the danger."

Danger? I couldn't figure out why she said mean things about Mr. Samuelian, and some others like light candlesfor everything people, too, for that matter. He had become my first pal after I moved in with my grandmother. I'd known him a little bit before, since whenever we used to visit Abuelita, my dad seemed like he preferred to be out talking with the neighbor than inside being ignored by Grandma. It was weird, because on those visits, she'd talk Spanish to Mom when Daddy was around, but she almost always spoke English when he wasn't.

Anyways, my grandmother said, "Help me pick some of these onions, mi'jito." We gathered a few from the garden, and she said, "Take those in, por favor. I must wring a hen's neck for dinner."

I was gathering the onions fast because I hated watching Abuelita kill chickens, but she called to me, "You forgot to wear a hat for your skin. You must always wear one, mi'jito." Complexion was real important to Abuelita.

My father had passed his fair skin to me, and my grand-mother seemed worried that I'd turn dark in the sun, although she was kind of dark herself.

Hey, I wanted to be brown so I wouldn't look so different from the other kids at school. But I put on the hat she'd bought me anyways; it was easier not to argue.

When I got back to the house, Abuelita announced, "Oh, there is a letter for you, mi'jito."

"From Daddy?" I said.

"No, of course not!" she snapped. "It is from your mother, who loves you."

"Oh," I said, and I picked up the envelope—it had already been opened—and took it onto the porch.

*My dearest Manuel,*

*My new job at the restaurant is good. I like the people I work with and I get the good meals there. I am saving as much money as I can so maybe you can come live with me soon. I still work at the drug store during the day too and I am living with tía Ysabel.*

*I hope you are being a good boy and obeying Abuelita and the nuns at Guadalupe. Be careful of that Armenian that lives next door because Abuelita says he is full of dangerous thoughts. Stay away from him please, Abuelita knows best.*

*I miss you every day and pray for the time when you can come live with me, I am saving as much money for us as I can.*

*All my love—*
*Mama*

Reading the letter made me feel like crying, and I took the little piece of blanket out of my drawer so I could hold it. After my father left, I'd moved in with my grandma, so Mom could leave to find work in Los Angeles. By the time she'd located a job, I was enrolled in the sixth grade at Our Lady of Guadalupe School, where I was the only Ryan in a class of Garcías and Gonzalezes and Jiménezes. Mama and Grandma decided that I should complete the academic year.

Summer came and Mama determined that L.A. was not a good place to raise me —"Too many gangs and drugs and violence." — so I remained with Abuelita. My mom tried to visit me as often as she could, but she had those two jobs. And my dad was working in the oil fields way up in Alaska, so he couldn't come see me at all.

I really didn't know why my folks and me weren't together. I don't know if I did something wrong or what. Nobody ever told me. I know that after he lost his job in the oilfields, Mama and daddy stopped laughing; before that, they giggled and tickled and stuff all the time.

They'd tell me to watch television, then they'd go in their bedroom, and I could hear their voices through the walls of our mobile home: "You can't expect me to leave my family and move all the way up there!"

"Helen, we're gonna lose this place. We're gonna be on the street! I've gotta work!"

"We can live with my family."

"No!" he hollered. "I've gotta have my own job. I won't take charity."

One day, I heard Mom talking to Abuelita. "Oh," the older woman said, "you would abandon your own mother for that Irish? I warned you not to marry one of los otros. They do not understand family. They move all around and never care for their mothers."

"I wouldn't leave you, Mama," my mother had said, "but what about Tuti?"

Tuti was my Uncle Arturo, Mama's older brother. He lived here in Bakersfield. He and Tía Gloria had two kids, and they seemed to live their own lives most of the time. Abuelita said mean things about Aunt Gloria, so her and Uncle Tuti didn't come around very often.

Abuelita waved the suggestion off. "Arturo never visits

his mother that gave him life. He acts like los otros, with his big, important gringo job. You are my only hope, m'ija. Please, please don't leave me for that Irish."

When we had returned home that day, Mama and Daddy had locked themselves in the bedroom again, and I'd heard through the walls. "My mother needs me here!"

"I need you!" He had once more visited the unemployment office in Bakersfield that day, but had only found that position far away.

Then one day Daddy was packing his stuff in cardboard boxes and piling them in the back of the old pickup he'd always used to go to work when he still had a job. He loaded his tools in the back too, and his fishing pole.

"Where're we going?" I asked.

"I got a new job, Manny, but it's way up in Alaska. I have to go alone for now." He looked away as he said that, then he continued, "When I get established, though, get our bills paid off, I'll send for you and Mama...if she'll come." He looked real sad.

We lived in a trailer park on the outskirts of Bakersfield then, and me and him walked away from it along a canal where we used to fish together.

"You're gonna be the man of the house now, Manny..." his voice sounded like he might even cry.

That made me feel like I might, too. "Why, Daddy? Why can't we all just go together?"

"I really don't know, son. I don't understand why either. You'll have to ask your mother about that. You've gotta be a man now. Protect Mama. I'm counting on you." Then he give me that bike.

Right after he left, my mother and me moved out of our trailer. She moved down to stay with my Aunt Ysabel in East Los Angeles, where she found work. Both my parents were gone then, and I started wetting the bed.

➤

## Chapter 6
# The Armenian

After I moved in with Abuelita, Mr. Samuelian seemed like he knew how much I missed Mama and Daddy, so he went out of his way to be friendly. That helped me get to know the neighborhood kids I hadn't already met, because most of them hung around his yard. He really acted like he enjoyed having us around, offering fruit from his trees and free run of his property, along with advice. Like Flaco's cussing: "You hold in your mouth what I scrape off my shoe." Flaco watched his language after that.

Because I lived next door, I saw more of the old poet than the other guys. He owned this little tiny shack on a narrow lot covered with old fruit trees and towering weeds, both of which he cultivated. As much as we all loved his fruit, it was his weeds that most attracted us, the very weeds my grandmother hated. They were *awesome*, a real jungle — thick and tall, flowered, feathered, short, wrinkled and sprawling everywhere. Some of them were higher than my head, and others were like carpet. Us kids had cut tunnels through the tall ones, and we'd crawl to play jungle. Everything on the yard, weeds and trees, was thick from water and fertilizer.

In fact, Mr. Samuelian probably wasn't as interesting to most kids as his yard, but to me he was. He was retired or something, and I knew that his wife had died before he'd even moved into our neighborhood and that he didn't have any kids. Each morning and evening, he cultivated his yard, sometimes spouting lines from poems as he worked, then stopping to jot them with the stub of a pencil into this little notebook he always carried.

He had these two friends, old guys like him, named Jefe and Ramón — one as dark as the black guys at school, the other as white as my dad. They had both been vaqueros, like my grandpa used to be, and they both still dressed like cowboys: boots, jeans, western shirts and these big battered sombreros. They'd drop by two or three times a week, always together. Sometimes they'd work in the yard with my neighbor. Other times the three of them would drink coffee, the cowboys smoking these drooping cigarettes they rolled themselves, and they'd talk. I used to love to listen because they told such great stories—sometimes even about my abuelo. "Hey, this kid he looks a little like old Manolo?" said Jefe one day. "And you're named after him, eh?" he said to me.

"I guess."

"Well, that's a good name you've got to live up to, Manolito," Jefe said to me. He'd never called me that before. He winked at Ramón, then he added, "You think he's tough as Manolo was?"

"I don't know...not many ever was as tough as him. But look at that skin. Old Manolo was as dark as this boy is light. To be Mexican sure don't have much to do with color, I think." He grinned and turned to Mr. Samuelian and said, "We used to say about this boy's abuelo, 'Ése no le debe ni los buenas días a los Españoles!'"

The men laughed.

"What's that mean?" I asked.

"That means...how you say it?...'That guy don't owe even a good morning to the Spaniards.' He wasn't much Spanish, your abuelo...or Irish either, I think. When I've worked south in Mexico, I've met lots of guys fairer than me. A lot of redheads in Sonora, eh Jefe? Your grandpa, he was a mixture like most of us, but mostly Indian I think...the color of an old saddle and tougher than one. I seen some guys that talked a purty good fight call him 'sir' without blinking. He was tough as a pigskin reata, Manolo, and a top hand."

It made me proud to hear them talk about my grandpa that way. I wanted to be tough as a pigskin reata, whatever that was, and a top hand.

But my grandma didn't like Ramón and Jefe for some reason, saying they were ruffians and drunks. She said they had never settled down "like respectable men," and they didn't go to church enough. But they seemed like real nice guys to me, and besides that, they told me that they used to sit with my abuelo on that old couch in front of the house before he died.

During the heat of summer and fall days, Mr. Samuelian would usually disappear into his little house, and we never disturbed him then. From my yard, I could hear the clatter of typewriter keys over the whir from the big old cooler on his roof. Once a week or so he'd walk to the bus stop down the street, balancing an armload of books to return to the public library. Then he'd be back with another load later.

"What's in those books?" Abuelita would demand, not of Mr. Samuelian, of course, but of me. "A person doesn't need all those books. Only the Holy Bible should be read. It is not natural for a man to read so much," she'd assert before I could answer, closing the discussion.

"How come you want me to read my school books

23

then?" I'd ask.

"Oh! Is that how you talk to your elders now that you go next door to the madman?"

Us kids knew what was in the books Mr. Samuelian read, or at least some of them, because he told us—something Abuelita suspected but could not prove.

"He talks to you," she would accuse.

"Sure," I'd reply, "about baseball. He thinks the Cubs'll win this year."

"Hah!" she would snort. "You'd better stay away from him. He is loco and he will twist you. You cannot trust los otros." My abuelita was too wise to absolutely forbid that I speak with our neighbor, but she kept a close eye on me.

We did discuss baseball, me and Mr. Samuelian, but only occasionally. The poet talked to us guys about lots of things — why the sky is no longer blue, how the tongue of a whale weighs as much as an elephant, what the Constitution guarantees, where the water we drink comes from — lots of stuff.

When some workers in the grape fields up north in Delano went on strike, my family — Mama, who was visiting, and Abuelita — agreed that the strikers and the priests supporting them were a bunch of communists. I didn't know for certain what communists were, but I could tell that they were real bad.

Later, I wandered next door to ask Mr. Samuelian if the strikers were communists and what it meant if they were.

His bushy eyebrows quivered like caterpillars dancing, and he handed me a pomegranate from his tree. "Look at it, my boy," he exclaimed, "a little leather pouch filled with rubies!" I giggled. "Now, who told you the people in the fields are communists?"

"Mama and Abuelita."

"Ah, and you don't know what 'communist' means?" He cleared his throat and plopped down onto the old wooden garden chair under a tree near his front door. "Well," he said, "it is one of those words with no precise meaning."

"I don't get it." I was pulling the leathery peel from the fruit he'd given me.

Mr. Samuelian smiled. "I mean, my boy, that people know the word has the power to hurt others, so they apply it to anyone or anything they don't like. People call the strikers that to discredit them. Do you understand?"

I wasn't certain I did. "Like calling someone a bad name?" I asked, after crunching a mouthful of the juicy red beads. Then I asked, "What about 'sticks and stones can break my bones, but words will never hurt me'?" I bit into the pomegranate once more and a crimson stream shot from the fruit.

Mr. Samuelian ducked quickly. "You are dangerous," he chuckled. "To answer your question, I'm afraid that words can hurt you far more than sticks and stones normally do. What if I go to your school and tell the teachers that you are a thief? That word not only means you have stolen, it predicts that you will steal again. You might suffer from the effects of that label, 'thief,' long after a broken bone had healed," he nodded.

"You mean like if some kids at school called you gabacho or gringo?"

"Do they call you that at school?"

"Sometimes."

He looked at me sadly for a moment, then continued, "Yes, words can hurt you. Use them carefully."

Impulsively, I asked, "What if someone said someone else was loco?"

A slight grin curved under Mr. Samuelian's mustache. "Well, it depends on who uses it. If said by a fool, it is dismissed. On the other hand, if a doctor says a person is crazy, that word can be a heavy burden." He spoke earnestly, then his tone brightened. "Fortunately, fools not doctors usually say such things. Check how many you hear say it are doctors."

"Oh," I said, because I caught on right away to what that made my grandmother. She sure wasn't a doctor.

Just then we heard a big ruckus — growling and snarling and barking — then around the corner sprinted Flaco's dog Rollo, moving so fast that it looked like sparks were flying from his feet; his legs were real blurry and his eyes were real big. Not too far behind him was Mrs. Molina's mongrel that us kids called 'Chuco, and he looked mad. I guess Rollo was busy trying not to have to beat 'Chuco up, or maybe 'Chuco hadn't heard how dangerous Flaco's pet was.

"Rollo he's supposed to be real tough," I said to Mr. Samuelian, shaking my head.

"He's pretty fast, too," grinned the old man.

## Chapter 7
# Evil Eye

That week me and Flaco and Keeny were working with Mr. Samuelian on a big birdhouse — "A hotel for our little friends," he called it.

"Friends!" huffed Grandma when I told her. "Those birds eat my garden. They leave the nasty white spots! First that crazy Armenian feeds them, and now he houses them. He is loco, I tell you!" She sounded mad.

"They're just birds, Abuelita," I pointed out.

"You have no idea the terrible damage they do. Like that mad Armenian, they are a menace."

What could I say? "Okay."

"I warn you and warn you! Avoid him. He is dangerous. Muy peligroso." She swayed for a moment like a big wind had caught her as she said that.

"Abuelita, are you okay?"

By then she was gripping the kitchen counter and taking a deep breath. "I am fine," she puffed, "but that Armenian is not. He is loco."

She sure didn't look fine to me.

Anyways, the next day us guys were working on the hotel for birds while Mr. Samuelian was at the library. Flaco and Keeny were arguing, as usual, over the best pro football team.

"Hey, ese, the Raiders always kick butt," asserted Flaco.

"Don't either, pendejo! The Forty-Niners rule!"

"Don't!"

"Do! 'Niners rule!"

"Don't!"

We were just finishing the birdhouse, them carrying on, when a large, dark sedan swooped into the dirt driveway. Our neighbor owned only an old bicycle as a vehicle, so I had rarely seen an automobile there.

A husky man who looked like Mr. Samuelian swung from the car's door. He was darker, like he worked outside all the time, but he had the same white hair, but with some black, and the same hook of a nose. His eyebrows were black, and he had a ferocious, mostly black mustache. One of his eyes was covered by a dark patch. "Hello, my lads!" he called. "Where is Sarkis Samuelian?"

"He went downtown to the library," I answered.

"Always reading. He will destroy his vision yet. And who are you young gentlemen?"

"I'm Manuel. I live next door. This is Flaco and Keeny."

"Well, young gentlemen, I am Haig Samuelian, brother of Sarkis Samuelian. And what do you work on?"

"It's just this birdhouse," Keeny answered.

"You appear to be smart lads, but be careful with those tools. See this ..." he tugged at the patch that covered his eye, "... a stray screwdriver can put your eye out!"

"Oh!" I said. I'd heard all my life about the variety of implements that might put an eye out, but this was my first contact with someone it had actually happened to.

Before I could ask about the eye, Mr. Samuelian walked up, toting a load of books. "Ahhh!" he called. "My baby brother visits! Why aren't you in Fresno counting your raisins?"

"Only a fool counts his raisins and ignores his grapes!" replied the one-eyed man, and he hugged Mr. Samuelian. "I've just been commiserating with your associates here."

"Oh," grinned our neighbor, "these young scamps. They're doing a fine job on the new birdhouse, aren't they. Come in, Haig, we must have coffee. How's Aram? Where is Malik's son now? And Dorothy? Still a dancer?"

They disappeared into the house. As soon as they were gone, Flaco said, "Ese! That old guy I think he got his you-know-what poked out."

"Simón!" agreed Keeny.

We livened up the rest of the afternoon discussing his poked eye. "I wonder what's left, ese? I wonder does he just got a hole there?" said Keeny.

"Maybe it's all dried up like Mrs. López's dried up old hand," said Flaco.

"Grossisimo!" It was a word we'd invented, so we giggled together.

"Maybe it's like that place where there use to be a boil on your brother Bruno's neck," I told Keeny.

"Grossisimo!" he said.

Before we went home that night, Haig Samuelian handed each of us a small bag of pomegranates. "Those are from Fresno, my lads. They are the finest in the world."

"Gee, thanks."

I took mine to Grandma, but she would not touch them. "You got these from that Armenian pirata?"

"From Mr. Samuelian's brother."

"His brother? He didn't praise you, did he?'"

"He said us guys were smart."

Abuelita staggered back a step. "Oh," she gasped, making the sign of the Cross. "He wants to steal your intelligence. Beware of him, with his mal de ojo. That is the sign of a brujo."

"*Mal de ojo*? Bad of eye?" A lot of the stuff she said

wasn't real clear to me. And she'd called him a brujo, a witch. I'd've laughed, but she seemed real serious.

"The evil eye, my son. He has the evil eye."

"Evil eye? Abuelita that's just Mr. Samuelian's brother..."

"Another of those Armenians!" she hissed.

"...and he got that eye poked out by a screwdriver."

"You are young," she told me. "You haven't seen behind that mask. You do not understand the realm of evil."

"The realm of evil?"

She stopped then and gazed directly at me. "If you ever look deeply into un mal de ojo you will see Hell itself."

"Hell itself?" I didn't have a clue what she was talking about. It seemed to me like she was losing her marbles.

"Pray your rosary," she cautioned.

"Okay."

"And don't be working outside in the sun without your hat," she added. "It is very important."

"How come?"

"I have told you and told you, that sun will make you dark como un cholo."

Like a cholo? That's the word the guys at school called the new kids who'd just come up from Mexico. She doesn't know this, but I hate being light so much that one day, when Abuelita wasn't home, I even put black shoe polish on my hair, but it looked real dopey. I had a heck of time washing it out before she got back.

"My friends Keeny and Flaco're dark, or kinda, anyways."

"Yes," she said, "they certainly are. Stay out of the sun, mi'jito. I don't want you to look like them."

Just then the phone rang. "Telephone," I said.

"Oh," said my grandma, "I wonder who that is?" She almost always said that before she answered.

"Oh, m'ija," Abuelita said into the receiver, "¿cómo estás? ¿Cómo estás mi hermana? ¿Y tu empleo?" She talked in Spanish for a long time, and I quit listening. Then she called me, "Mi'jito, tu mamá."

I took the receiver. "Hi, Mama."

"Hi honey? How are you?"

"Fine. Guess what? Mr. Samuelian's brother, he's visiting, and he's only got one eye. He wears one of those pirate patches too."

"Oh," she said, "I hate those things. Did your bicycle ever turn up?"

"No. That policeman he never even called back."

"I'm sorry to hear that. Well, maybe you'll get a new one some day."

"That'd be neat."

"How's school?"

"It's okay."

She chuckled and said, "You don't sound too enthused."

"I got Sister Blanche this year."

"Is she a good teacher?"

"She's okay. I'm getting 'A's, mostly."

"That's good, m'ijo. Study hard so you'll be able to get a good job when you grow up...." Then her voice changed and she added..., "not like me." My mother hadn't finished high school, I knew, and she always urged me to take advantage of my opportunities, maybe go on to college like Uncle Tuti had.

"Okay."

"Have you had any letters from Daddy?"

"No," I said, and I felt real sad all of a sudden.

Her voice changed and she said, "That's strange. He wrote to me once, and I can't imagine that he wouldn't write to you."

"He never comes to see me either," I added.

31

"He can't do that because he's too far away. But it's odd that he hasn't even written to you."

After we hung up, my grandma said, "Come, we will light a candle for your mother," and she managed to squeeze one more onto the shelf.

That night I had the dream again. I was lost in a great big white place, all ice and stuff, like giant snow-cones without syrup. I was real scared and I kept calling my dad, but my voice just echoed. No one ever answered.

When I woke up the next morning, the room was hot and my bed was soaked. I had to tell Abuelita that I'd had an accident, but she didn't get mad or anything. Instead, she just shrugged, "No matter mi'jito, it is God's will," and she patted my cheek with a hand smooth as porcelain. "There is nothing soap and water cannot wash out."

When she acted like that, I really loved her.

## Chapter 8
# The Bully

After breakfast I couldn't wait to slip over to our neighbor's yard, maybe steal a glance behind that eye-patch. The large car was still there but its owner wasn't in sight, so I helped Mr. Samuelian. While staking up peas, he busied himself reciting his latest verse — "Great unconquered wilderness is calling, calling me! It's crystal peaks and wooded glens all yearn to set me free!"

Before long, the brother with a hole in his face emerged from the small house and began picking and sampling ripe plums from a tree in the overgrown yard.

"These are wonderful," he said, "almost as good as the ones in Fresno." After a moment, his tone deepened and his eye fixed on me: "You see those sharp stakes. Beware of them! My eye..." he said heavily, pulling at his patch.

I gulped, thinking then of Tuxedo the cat and his milky eye, pecked by the rooster.

Later that day, me and Flaco and Keeny were erecting the bird hotel — Flaco telling us he had to tie Rollo up because he was beating up too many neighborhood dogs — when this big kid named David Avila, who had chased us home from school more than once, he came swaggering up the block, then he stood on the dirt border between the yard and the rutted street. A week earlier he'd caught me after school, wrestled me to the ground, and given me a Dutch rub and a pink belly too; he especially like to pound my pale skin because it turned red so easy. Avila looked to me like a big brown toad. He had real biceps, though, and the beginnings of a mustache. He was only a grade ahead of us at Our Lady of Guadalupe School, but he was already a teenager.

Anyways, the big toad, he kind of studied us, sneered, then hollered, "Hey leettle pendejos, I can't wait for them birds. I got me a B-B gun and I weel keel them all. Maybe I weel shoot you three leettle pendejos too. You just wait!"

"No, you just wait, young criminal!" I heard a shout and Mr. Samuelian's brother dashed from the plum tree's foliage—I don't think Avila had noticed him there. In a moment, he had the bully by the neck and was shaking him with one hand while he thrust an open wallet into his face with the other.

"Do you see this badge?" he demanded. "I'll have you in jail for years if you bring a B-B gun around here! Do you understand? Do you see this patch? A B-B gun!" He shook Avila again.

The bully wilted quickly under Haig Samuelian's storm and he sprinted away as soon as the one-eyed man let him go.

"Scalawag!" Haig shouted after him. "Scoundrel!" he continued fuming as he returned, his fierce mustache twitching. "I can have him jailed!" He thrust his wallet toward us and displayed a small badge with "Friend of the Fresno County Sheriff's Department" printed on it.

"Ah, Haig! Haig!" called Mr. Samuelian, walking from his pea patch to pound his brother's broad back. "Ever the crusader, Haig!"

Just then Jefe and Ramón, ambled up, glancing back at the running Avila. "¿Qué pasó?" asked Jefe.

After my neighbor described the clash, Jefe smiled and said, "Su hermano es muy caballero."

"De veras," added Ramón

"Yes," smiled Mr. Samuelian, "he is something."

"B-B guns!" muttered Haig Samuelian, and he spat vehemently on the ground and jerked his patch momentarily. Then he shook hands with his brother's friends.

"Come," urged Mr. Samuelian, "let me give you a glass of tea, Haig, Ramón, Jefe," and the men entered the small house.

"I bet it's a glass eye under that patch, ese," said Keeny. "I tried to look under when he was pickin' plums but I couldn't see nothin'."

"I think it's a big hole, ese," suggested Flaco, "with blood and pus."

"With worms, too, maybe," I added. "I'll bet there's big worms in it."

"Grossisimo!" chorused my pals, and we laughed.

When I arrived home later, my grandma was talking to Mrs. Alcalá. "Esperanza, you didn't actually eat the pomegranates that brujo gave you?" Abuelita demanded.

"Of course," smiled Mrs. Alcalá. "They were delicious...all the way from Fresno. And he's not a brujo, Lupe, he's just another Samuelian, a gentleman but...ah...very enthusiastic."

"Enthusiastic?"

"And very friendly," added Mrs. Alcalá.

"Two of those Armenians now," my grandma said. "Both of them loco. And they probably both read books!"

Mrs. Alcalá was smirking when she added, "The Samuelians aren't the only locos in this neighborhood."

"And what is that supposed to mean, Esperanza?"

"Oh nothing," replied the old woman, grinning as she hobbled away on her canes. "Hasta la vista, Lupe."

"Oh!" fumed my grandmother. "I'm going to get her told!"

That long, warm evening the Samuelian brothers sat in wooden lawn chairs talking and slapping occasional mosquitoes. After Grandma freed me from chores, I wandered over to listen.

"That was the day I fought Dikran Nizibian, the terror. Remember, Sarkis? I fought him for an hour and fifteen minutes non-stop, the longest and fiercest battle in the history of Fresno. We fought all the way up Van Ness Avenue to Blackstone, and then we fought for miles down Blackstone. Our sweat flowed through the gutters. The police stood back in awe to watch such a battle. Businesses closed. Priests held crosses to their hearts. Doctors averted their eyes. Strong women prayed. Strong men fainted."

"Who won? Who won?" I asked, breathless.

"Who won?" he paused. Mr. Samuelian's brother twitched his mustache and tugged his patch. "I'll tell you who won. Do you see this eye?" he pointed at the cloth covering his empty socket. "The evil Dikran Nizibian tried to gouge it out in the middle of Blackstone Street in Fresno, but ...," another pause, another twitch, another tug ..., "he regrets it to this day because I knew a secret: Never use more when less will do! Never use two when one will do! I had saved my final strength. With it, I threw the ruthless Nizibian from me and broke everything on him that could be broken. I broke several things that could not be broken. He never fought again, did he Sarkis?"

"Not that I remember," replied Mr. Samuelian.

"He never bullied anyone again."

"Not that I remember."

"Nizibian the terror was finished," Haig Samuelian nodded with finality, pulling absently at his patch.

"Gouged out," I mumbled as I wandered home.

## Chapter 9
# "The Chase"

The next day at school, when I told my pals the story of the great Fresno fight, their jaws drooped like their baggy pants.

"No lie?" they gasped.

"I think Mr. Samuelian's brother he's a bad vato."

Flaco winked at Keeny, "Ryan said 'vato.'"

I ignored him.

By the time classes were over that day, though, Flaco was on a roll. "Yeah, well I'm gonna be a fighter when I grow up. I'm gonna be just like Julio Cesar Chavez, ese," he said, sort of bouncing like those spring dolls some people put in their cars.

"You aren't tough," said Keeny.

"Hey, I beat up Bernal one time."

"When?" I demanded.

"In second."

"Second grade?" I said, "That's not a fight, that's babies pushing each other."

"Hey, Ryan, you better watch it," he said, bouncing again, and snuffing his nose as he faked punches.

"I'll get you a match with Avila," I said.

"Oh yeah! Well, I bet I could take him. I got the speed!

I got the moves!" He windmilled his arms and did a couple of silly dance steps, looking like a clown to me.

I started chuckling.

"What're you laughin' at, ese?"

By then, Keeny was cracking up, too.

"Oh, nothing," I said. "Let's go to Mr. Samuelian's"

Flaco kind of grumbled for awhile — "I bet I really could take him." — on our way, but eventually we started talking about that pit that had been gouged in Haig Samuelian's face by the evil Nizibian, and hoping to at least catch a glimpse of it. Then we spied David Avila striding toward us.

"Hey Flaco," I said, "here's your chance to..." Flaco was gone. Him and Keeny both were sprinting away. I took off in a different direction in the hope the bully might be confused.

Unfortunately for me, he wasn't. As almost the only blond at Guadalupe School, it seemed like I was always Avila's favorite target. I didn't feel honored by that. I didn't have time to feel anything but scared because I was too busy running, looking like Rollo when 'Chuco chased him. That toad was after me. Although I was carrying my slingshot, I never considered using it because I was too busy running.

I was pretty fast for a sixth-grader, and I got even faster with David Avila on my tail, so at first I kept him way behind me. But I was juggling my book bag, sprinting and glancing back, sprinting and glancing back. Pretty soon I realized that Avila the terror was closing the gap between us, his toad eyes slit with evil plans for me. I worked even harder to escape, but my breath was growing shallow and my thighs were tightening.

I shot another look behind me and he was so near that I saw the shadow of a mustache on his upper lip and the pink pimples, decorating his chin like small strawberries.

My breath was burning and my knees couldn't seem to lift anymore. That book bag swung wildly from side to side — I didn't have the energy to control it.

Just as I turned the corner of my block, I lost control of the bag and it dropped from my shoulder, spilling its contents on the street. I was nearly safe, but if I didn't pick up my books I might never see them again. Avila — the evil Avila — was right behind me.

Hesitating over my books and papers, I glimpsed back despondently, ready for the twisted arm, the dutch rub, the pink belly, or even the punches that were certain. Then I realized that Avila had halted. He'd thrust his hands into his pockets and turned away, his shoulders low as a real toad's. Turning back, I saw the one-eyed Samuelian standing in front of his brother's yard, hands on hips, glaring at David Avila. When I peered once more at the bully, he was retreating in a hurry.

I was so relieved that I almost forgot to pick up my books and papers. After I finally did, though, I hurried to our neighbor's house. The large car was being loaded with a suitcase, and Haig Samuelian said to me, "Remember, never use more when less will do, and that young hoodlum will soon learn to leave you alone."

Then the two older men returned to what seemed to be a conversation in progress. "No matter, Sarkis," the younger brother said. "I'll pass the message on to Aram. He will understand." The men hugged, then Haig Samuelian noticed what I carried and said, "Don't let this young man play with that sling shot. You remember my eye, don't you?" He pointed toward his covered eye-socket as he swung into the driver's seat.

His brother smiled, "I remember."

"Well, I must be on my way. I have grapes to tend in Fresno." The two brothers shook hands. The larger man tugged his patch and smiled out the window as he started the engine. "Farewell, young man," he said to me.

I didn't reply because I'd noticed something a second before when Haig Samuelian had tugged at his small mask while sitting there, his face nearly level with mine. I noticed that there was no untanned skin beneath the patch or the string that tied it.

No untanned skin.

Beneath the wrist watch Abuelita had given me last Christmas my own surface was pale as a baby's. Then I began to realize what that had to mean: "You been changin' eyes!" I thought aloud.

"What is that?" the driver inquired.

"Your patch, it's on the other eye. You been changin' eyes. You been changin' every day."

Haig Samuelian lifted his patch and winked with a twinkling eye I thought I'd never seen before, and said to his brother, "Beware of this one, Sarkis. He will go places."

Then he drove north toward Fresno.

## Chapter 10
# Friends

The only thing that made my sixth grade year at Guadalupe any fun was when I got this big package from my dad at Christmas. I was standing in front of the house on the first day of vacation when a United Parcel truck drove up. The man said he had a package for Manuel Ryan, and when I said that was me, he handed it over.

A second later, Abuelita wandered out and asked, "What is that?"

"It's this package a man just delivered for me."

"For you?"

"Yeah, and it says here that my dad sent it all the way from Alaska. I bet it's a present."

"Oh," she'd said, then disappeared into the house almost like she was mad.

When I finally got to open the box at Christmas, it was this awesome leather jacket with a real fur collar. And there was a cool Christmas card too that showed a totem pole. It said, "To Manny, with love, from Dad."

Mostly, though, school really seemed to drag that year. I kept having those "accidents" at night, even though I tried as hard as I could not to, but Abuelita never even mentioned them. She was real nice. She had this old-fashioned washing machine with a wringer and stuff, and she'd just wash my sheets, then hang them out to dry on the clothes line in back of the house. And I never, never told any of my friends at school about the "accidents."

Anyways, summer finally arrived. Avila the terror disappeared then, so I didn't have to keep hiding out. Momma came to visit a few times and I traveled to L.A. when she had a vacation. She took me to Disneyland and to the beach, too. And she phoned me every week.

But I didn't hear anything else from my dad. One evening I was talking to my mother on the telephone and she asked if Grandma seemed like she was sick, or maybe dizzy, very much. I said, no, not really. I'd seen her grab the sink once or twice, and one day she looked real strange while she was watching T.V., but I couldn't remember any other times.

"Let me talk to Abuelita, m'ijo." Soon after my grandmother took the phone, I heard her say, "Go to the doctor! Why bother? He cures nothing and charges me all my money!" she spat. "If I get sick, I'll see Manuela Aldrete, the curandera. Not the doctor!"

"Go outside for a minute, mi'jito," she ordered, and I knew she didn't want me to hear what they were saying. I grabbed my little shred of a blanket, walked out to the old couch and plopped onto it. I couldn't make out what was being said inside, but the tone of my grandmother's voice through the thin walls told me they were arguing about something. I was thinking that now I was going to lose my grandma just the way I lost my mom and dad. I held my little piece of blanket in one pocket so nobody could see, and I felt almost like crying. This really sucks, I thought, because it was like the fights before my dad left.

I noticed Mr. Samuelian working in his yard, weeding his weeds I think, so I walked over.

He smiled at me, then asked, "What's wrong Manuel?"

42

"My mom lives in L.A. and my dad lives in Alaska and I live here and nobody even likes me."

He stood and wiped his hands, then patted my back. "Well, I like you. So do Flaco and Keeny and your other school friends. Your mother and your father and your grandmother more than like you. Don't be fooled by some of their actions."

He sat on one of the rickety old wooden lawn chairs and motioned me to sit on one. "You know, Manuel, being a grownup can be difficult too. When you are young, it looks like adults can do anything they want, but they can't. Although I barely know your parents, I can assure you that they are doing what they believe is right. And your grandmother is doing what she believes is best for you. They are all doing their best."

"Then why aren't we together?"

He smiled sadly. "Because no one agrees on what is best. Sooner or later they will, but it is hard for you now, I know."

Just then I heard some loud squawking and saw that some of Abuelita's hens had wandered to that dirt border between our yard and the road. Rollo had spied them and was chasing them back into the yard. I jumped up to stop him just as Taco, my grandma's rooster, rounded the house at a run, kind of bouncing that funny chicken way, but he wasn't playing.

The rooster's feathers were standing up, his wings were extended, and his head looked huge, ten times bigger than usual. When Rollo saw him, he slammed on the brakes and skidded, his hips sliding in front of his head as he tried to turn around, but Taco was too fast. He leapt, poking and pecking and scratching, raising a big cloud of dust.

Everything was happening so fast I couldn't tell for sure what was going on, but I sure heard the dog yip, then Rollo was sprinting for home.

Taco didn't chase him, but instead he kind of fluffed his feathers and jerked his head, then let out with a real loud cock-a-doodle-do, his wings flappping and neck streatched way out. Just as my grandma came out the front door of our house to see what had happened, the rooster jumped on one of the hens like he was spanking her.

Mr. Samueilan grinned and shook his head, saying, "That dog doesn't learn does he?"

"Neither does his owner," I replied.

"Manuel! ¡Ven aqui!" I heard Abuelita shout, and I looked up. She was standing in the doorway. "You come home now!"

"I gotta go," I said.

"Don't give up," smiled our neighbor. "They all love you."

I only nodded and fingered the little piece of blanket in my pocket. They had awful funny ways of showing it if they did.

When I returned home, my grandmother said, "I told you not to talk to that Armenian."

"Yes, Abuelita," I replied. Right then I didn't care what she'd told me.

# Chapter 11
# Alphabet

The new school year started that next week, and I was in junior high at last. I made up my mind that I wouldn't have any more accidents. I was getting too old for that stuff. And if my folks weren't going to come back, then I'd just have to grow up and take care of myself.

At Guadalupe, the junior high kids — us seventh-graders and the eighth-graders, too — were still in the same building as the primary kids, but it was better. We got some elective classes — I took Spanish — and we got to help tutor the little kids, to show them basketball and stuff. Besides, our new rooms had doors that opened out to the playground and basketball courts. Best of all, though, we got to use these cool computers.

There were some new kids in our class, too: a real pretty girl named Linda Garcia and two guys named Nguyen — Tran (we called him Alphabet) and Phuc (we had a nasty nickname for him), but they weren't brothers or anything. In fact, all of sudden there were Nguyens in all the classes it seemed like — and Truongs, Trans and Vangs and even one girl named Nhouyvanusong (the other kids called her "Jawbreaker"), and Flaco he claimed there was this Vietnamese gang in town now, but I never saw one. Anyways, I tried to be real friendly with all the new kids because I remembered how I'd felt the year before when I'd been one.

Us guys took notice of Phuc Nguyen first because Tony Zepeda, a kind of small bully who liked to pick on other little guys, he called the new kid the F-word at lunch the second day of school, and he laughed at him. Phuc Nguyen kicked Tony between the legs, hit him on the nose, then kicked him on the ear, ending the fight fast. Everybody was dazzled. Afterwards, Zepeda said through his bloody nose that he was really gonna get Phuc, but he retired from fighting after that, and stayed away from him. The new kid never even talked about Tony.

Tran he liked sports, so me and him hit it right off. He was the best athlete of all the new kids that transferred in, and he looked different than the others, too —bigger, darker, and with hair that was real wavy. Anyways, after school on the second day, me, Flaco and Keeny were playing H-O-R-S-E basketball with him. He could really shoot. In fact, he was winning easy. "Boy," I said, "I sure hope you got out for the team, Alphabet."

Before he could answer, I heard Flaco say, "Oh, oh!" and when I looked up, Avila the bully was striding across the playground straight toward us. I gulped because I figured I was still his favorite target.

"Let's haul ass, ese," urged Flaco, and he did haul it, pronto, with Keeny hot on his heels. Since I'd checked the ball out, I couldn't leave, though I really wanted to sprint away with my pals.

Tran hadn't been at Guadalupe long enough to know that danger was coming toward us, so he remained with me. "What it means, this ese?" he asked.

"I don't know for sure," I said nervously, "but all the dudes around here say it." My eyes were riveted on the Avila. "Maybe 'guy' or something."

"My shoot?" asked Tran. His English wasn't real good yet.

I didn't reply because by then Avila had already swaggered close enough to knock the ball out of my hands, almost taking my hands with it. "Hey, pendejo," he grunted, "I'll show you how." All his "sh" sounds came out sounding like "ch," and vice versa. Me and Keeny and Flaco liked to make fun of how he talked when he wasn't around.

He fired up an air ball. "I meesed on purpose," he growled. "What're you laughin' at, you leettle Chinaman?" (His last word sounded like "shine-a-man," but I sure didn't laugh at him.)

"Shoot bad," Tran replied pleasantly.

I tried to give my new friend a high sign to shut him up, but he just stood there smiling. He was almost as skinny as me, an easy target for the muscular Avila.

"Theenk eets fonny?" demanded the toad, and he threw the ball hard at Tran's face. The new kid's hands came up so quick that I almost didn't see them; he caught the projectile, then swished it through the net.

For a second even Avila blinked, then he demanded, "You want me to keeck your bott?" He pushed Tran's chest, sending the thin kid across the paved court.

Tran stopped, held his arms stiffly at his sides, and glared at the toad. "No push," he warned.

"Leave him alone, Avila," I said.

"You want your leetle bott keecked too, gabacho?" he glowered at me.

"What's going on over there," demanded Sister Mary Charles from across the playground. She was after-school monitor. "You aren't playing rough are you David Avila?"

"Who, me? No seester," the toad smiled. As soon as her gaze left him, he hissed to us, "I'll get you two leetle pendejos. Just you wait. I'll keeck both your botts." He turned then and swaggered toward the street.

"You shouldn't've stood up to him like that," I said.

"No push me," said Alphabet, and he sounded real

serious.

"He's a bad-ass," I said.

"No push me," Tran repeated. "Nobody push me."

I was afraid Avila would beat him up for sure if he caught him away from school.

By that evening I'd forgotten that stuff, and I said to Abuelita, "We got these computers at school now. They're real fun."

"I don't know anything about those computers," she said, and her nose seemed to curl up.

"Do you think we might...buy...one?" I asked.

She faced me and explained, "We are not rich, hijo. Even with the money your mother sends me, we are not rich. Those computers they are for los ricos not for common people like us. Common people like us do not need such...gadgets."

Common people? Gadgets? I wasn't sure what she meant, but I knew we weren't going to buy a computer, that much was for sure. Oh well, I didn't really expect her to say yes.

➤

Chapter 12
# What's Natural?

"Know what, Abuelita? There's this new kid in my class named Tran Nguyen and he's real good at basketball and real smart too. I like him."

"Tran Nguyen? What kind of name is that?"

"Him and his mom came from Vietnam."

"From Vietnam? Oh, they are Orientals. He is an Oriental boy is he?" She paused, seeming to think then said, "Be careful, mi'jito, those Orientals are muy distinto. Do not play too much with him." She shook her head and mumbled, "Los otros, more all the time, and Esperanza Alcalá says I am worried over nothing. I'm going to tell her off one of these days."

Actually, my grandma told Mrs. Alcalá off all the time, but our neighbor never heard her because Abuelita never thought of what to say while Mrs. Alcalá was present. I was the only one who got to hear her. "God wants people to stay with their own kind, not to mix mi'jito!" she huffed to me that night. "It isn't natural to mix. Do birds play with snakes? Do they marry and have children? No. Those Orientals should stay with other Orientals, the Armenians with the Armenians, the Negroes with the Negroes. The Bible forbids mixing. It is not natural." She nodded her head like she'd settled things.

"Jefe and Ramón they said my abuelo was mostly

Indian," I told her.

Her eyes flared, and Abuelita snapped, "My husband was pure Castillian! Oh, he was a little darker than me...from working in the sun...but pure Spanish. Do not listen to those two borrachos. They are liars!" She kind of spit that last word — real spit, wet stuff — and I knew I'd made her mad.

"Okay," I said. But I didn't really know what to believe. My father's family had been Irish and something. I wasn't exactly sure what because he never talked about it. His mom and dad had died when he was little, so I guess he was an orphan. Anyways, I knew Abuelita hadn't wanted my mother to marry him. She never exactly said that to me, but it was easy to figure out.

After dinner that evening I snuck over to Mr. Samuelian's yard as soon as I could. He was sitting in one of his wooden chairs, reading.

"How is junior high school, Manuel?" he asked after I sat next to him.

"It's pretty cool. We got these computers in our classroom and they're fun."

"Ah, they have those at the library too. You should join me one day. And your teacher?"

I made a face. "Me and Flaco and Keeny got Mr. Mancuso. He's wearing a wig this year, ese," I told him.

"Ese?" he said smiling, and I blushed because that "in" word had felt funny even while I was saying it to a grown-up.

"It's not a dirty word," I said rapidly.

Mr. Samuelian's grin widened. "I know, I know. It's just that I haven't heard you use it before. It's a perfectly good word, but one I associate with Flaco and Keeny."

I wasn't certain I wanted to use it any more, so I changed the subject. "Mr. Mancuso scratches his wig all the time so it gets crooked like a hat."

Mr. Samuelian grinned under his mustache, then said, "Well, we all have our vanities. When you are fifty years old, decide if Mr. Mancuso's are quite that funny. What's on your mind, Manuel? I can see by your expression that something troubles you."

"Well...," I didn't know exactly how to explain, "my grandma she says maybe I shouldn't play with this new kid that came to my school."

"Why is that?"

"She says he's an Oriental and it isn't natural for different kinds of people to be together. She says the Bible says not to."

"Oh." He closed his book.

"She says birds don't play with snakes or marry them and stuff, so it's not natural."

"Ah," he smiled, "but you do play with your new friend, right?"

"Sure," I nodded.

"Then it must be natural."

"Huh?" I wasn't certain I understood what he was saying.

"Do a bird and a snake play together?"

"Naw."

"That's not natural; they belong to different species. But you and your friend do play together, so it must be natural. You are both people, but a snake isn't a bird."

"Ohhh," I understood.

"Can a bird and a snake marry and have babies together?" he asked.

I giggled, "Naw...except maybe in cartoons." That was silly.

"They can't because that's not natural," our neighbor smiled. "Can a black man like Mr. Lawrence and a white woman like Mrs. Lawrence marry and have children?"

That seemed silly too. The Lawrences had about ten

51

kids. "Sure," I said.

"Then that is natural, Manuel. Nature allows it. Some people may not like it, but it is natural."

"But what about the Bible?" I asked.

"Oh, the Bible doesn't say anything in particular about such matters, but many people like to say things and claim the Bible supports them."

I was still troubled. "But my grandma..."

"Your grandmother is a good woman, but we all make mistakes, Manuel, no shame in that. Perhaps your grandmother made a small mistake." Then he added, "There is only shame if we don't learn from our errors."

"Oh."

"Have an apricot," he urged.

As I wandered home, Flaco and Keeny approached from the other direction. Each was wearing an old work glove on one hand, and Flaco carried a small bottle and a tennis ball. "Hey, ese," Flaco kind of whispered, glancing both ways like he had a big secret or something, "can you sneak out after dark? Me and Keeny're gonna go to the park and play fire-ball."

"Fire-ball?"

"Yeah, it's bad, ese. My cousin in L.A. he showed me. You take some gasoline" — he shook the small bottle — "and you put it all over a tennis ball, then light it and play catch. It looks just like a shootin' star, ese. No lie."

"Come on, Manuel," urged Keeny, "don't puss."

"You guys only got two gloves," I said. "You'll burn your hands."

Flaco made a face. "Essssse," he dragged the word out, "don't be chicken."

"I'm doing my homework," I said. I guess I was just getting tired of all Flaco's little-kid schemes, but I wasn't interested. "See you guys."

"Homework? Don't be a brown-noser," Flaco said,

more to Keeny than to me. He liked to say things like that just out of earshot, then claim he'd said them to someone's face.

I stopped. "Hey, Flaco, your nose is brown, ese, so just shut up!"

"Oh yeah! Yours is pink!"

"So what?" I demanded.

"So go do your homework, pendejo. We're gonna have fun!"

"I will, pendejo, so don't worry."

They watched me return to my house, then went on their way, Flaco talking as soon as he was sure I couldn't hear what he said. I still liked them, but I had other friends now who didn't always have to pretend they were tough, or pick arguments and stuff.

Sleeping that night, I wandered over the frigid land searching for my father. Even the sky was white, and it was like being suspended in those little crystal balls with water in them that you shake to make fake snow fly: I was just floating and calling my dad, floating and calling. I jolted awake just as I started to wet, so I climbed from bed and made it to the bathroom.

Even though it was still plenty dark, I thought I wouldn't be able to sleep anymore, but pretty soon I kind of drifted and there was my mother, but she looked strange, like she was crying and crying and wandering all over this desert. I tried to help her, but I felt like I was tied up or something. I couldn't reach her.

I woke up wet.

I ran into Flaco and Keeny on the way to school, and each wore a bandage on one hand. They looked like this picture of an old-time Chinese guy in our geography book because they didn't have any eyebrows or eyelashes. When I asked them what happened, they wouldn't tell me. "How was the fire-ball?" I asked.

"It was real cool, huh, Keeny?"

Keeny looked at Flaco strangely and hesitated, then said, "I guess...," like he wasn't too sure.

No one said anything for a minute, then I told them about that weird new dream, the one with my Mom in it.

Flaco's hairless eyes opened wide, and he said, "Hey, that wasn't your mom, ese, that was la Llorona, huh, Keeny."

"Simón cabrón," my other pal nodded.

"Who?" I asked.

"La Llorona, this lady that she killed her babies, ese, and now she's haunted. She's just lookin' and lookin' everywhere for those babies, huh, Keeny?"

"Simón. My abuela she told me that la Llorona could suck your soul out, ese." He crossed himself. "Swear to God," he added.

I'd heard more ghost stories since I started living in this neighborhood than all the rest of my life combined. Way back when I was little, my dad told me all that kind of stuff was fake, and I believed him, but these guys were serious. "Hey, it was my mother, guys," I told them. "I saw her. It wasn't any ghost."

"You better go get some holy water, huh, Keeny?"

"Simón."

"Right," I said. I wished I'd never even mentioned it. Besides, the more I thought about that dream it reminded me of this story Sister Cecilia had told us in sixth grade when she was substituting, about this guy named Eddie Puss that put his own eyes out because he lost his mom and dad or something like that. He was a famous king, but I suppose Flaco thought somebody stole that guy's soul too, took it to a used-soul lot to sell it.

Chapter 13
# A Lesson

During religion class at Guadalupe School the next day, I asked Mr. Mancuso if the Bible could be used to prove stuff that wasn't true. The question seemed to surprise him, and he scratched his new hair for a moment, then said, "Well, perhaps some religions do that, but we Catholics don't." I was thinking that my grandmother was the most Catholic person I knew, and it seemed like she claimed the Bible justified every opinion she had, no matter what it was.

David Avila, sitting at the rear of class, laughed aloud. He had flunked again, and was in my room now, but his attendance was poor, so I hadn't even realized he was present that day.

The teacher adjusted his wig, then said, "Mr. Avila go to the board and write the answers for today's homework, please."

Eyes on the floor, the bully rose from his desk and mumbled, "I don' got eet. My...ah...my leetle brother he...he ate eet."

"Go to the office," snapped Mr. Mancuso, and Avila, winking and grinning, swaggered out the door, but his eyes locked for a moment on the new kid, Tran Nguyen, who was laughing.

"I bet Avila gets kicked out this time, ese," whispered Flaco, poking me with his unbandaged hand. He held the other one away from his body. "We better really watch out for him now. He'll be mad."

"No lie, ese," added Keeny. He, too, favored his bandaged hand.

Flaco had told everyone in class that he'd hurt himself saving a lady from a burning house, and some of the dumb kids even believed him. Keeny had said simply, "Me too." I don't know exactly what had happened, but I could make a good guess. Besides, I really liked their missing eyebrows. That was way cool.

As our last class was finishing that day, Mr. Mancuso called my name: "Ryan! See me before you leave today."

"Oh-oh, ese," hissed Flaco, "you're in dutch now." He sounded delighted.

"Wait up for me after class, ese," I said. "We can play fire-ball on the way home."

Flaco grimaced, "Ha ha, Ryan. Very funny."

I thought it was. Anyway, after everyone else had left, I stood in front of Mr. Mancuso's desk. "Yes sir?" I said.

"You handed in this form, but it isn't filled out properly. Someone has crossed off 'Other' where it says 'Other Hispanic.' You need to take it home and have your grandmother look at it again."

"Yes sir."

As soon as I got outside, I crossed off the maimed "Other Hispanic" and put a check on "Mexican-American/Chicano." It didn't seem important enough to fiddle with.

After another game of H-O-R-S-E with Tran that afternoon — he won as usual — I walked with him toward the little store his mother operated. About half-way there, though, Avila suddenly appeared nearly beside us from a vacant lot. He had two smaller guys with him, one we called Mosquito and the other one we called Scuffs. They liked to pretend they were tough.

Come on!" I urged Alphabet, but he didn't seem to want to run.

I immediately hunched over, ready to be beaten up, but Avila marched right past me and confronted my new friend. "You theenk I'm fonny, you leetle Chinaman?"

"Not Chinaman," Tran said.

"You call me a liar, pendejo Chinaman?"

"You liar," replied Alphabet without flinching.

I was thinking, *Don't say that*, Alphabet. Don't say that. "He didn't really mean it, Avila," I said quickly.

"Shut up man," Mosquito snapped at me.

I started to say something, but Avila had already launched a wide punch. It sailed toward Tran, but by the time it arrived, the slim boy had dodged and Avila was off-balance. Almost before I realized what had happened, Alphabet kicked the bully two, three times in the belly and chest, then danced out of range.

Wow! I'd never seen anyone move so fast.

"Cabrón!" cried the toad. And he surged forward, but Tran dodged aside and kicked him again, clear up near the ear this time, then punched him twice.

The bully again roared "Cabrón!" and he once more attacked and once more he was kicked and kicked and kicked again, then punched by the thinner, faster boy. I was dazzled. I'd never seen anything like this before: David Avila, the menace, was actually being beaten up, and by a kid my size.

Then I noticed Mosquito edging around behind Tran, so I dashed toward him and said, "Better leave him alone, ese. If you wanta fight, fight me."

When he realized I was serious, and that Avila couldn't help him, Mosquito said, "I gotta go home," and off he hurried with Scuffs right behind him.

While I was watching them leave, I heard several more fast "Smacks!" and when I turned Avila stood weaving slightly, his fists lower, his chest heaving. He was bruised and lumped from the kicks and punches he'd endured, and now he was outnumbered, but he wasn't quitting. "Come on, pendejos," he challenged. "I'll beat both of you."

"Why you fight me?" demanded Alphabet, who still appeared fresh and fast.

"You, all you pendejo teachers' pets," he puffed. "I'll get you."

"Hey, Avila," I said, "we never did anything to you. You started it."

"You pendejos with your A's. You make fun of me."

"You could get A's if you'd quit ditching school and do your homework," I said.

"Come on, chickens," challenged Avila, and he put his head down and charged, trying once more to overwhelm Tran with roundhouse punches, only to be kicked and hit until he fell groaning to the ground.

"Don't hit him anymore, okay Alphabet?" I urged. All of a sudden I didn't want to see Avila or anyone else beaten up. I began to wonder if maybe Avila acted so mean because he thought it was the only why he *could* act.

"Let's go, okay," I urged.

"Why you want fight me?" Tran demanded.

Avila didn't reply.

After only another moment's hesitation, Tran turned and the two of us walked away, leaving Avila on the vacant lot.

From across the street I heard a woman call, "What's going on over there, you boys?"

We didn't answer.

That evening I told Mr. Samuelian about the battle. "Honest," I said, "this new kid named Tran I told you about before, he's not real big or anything, but he beat up David Avila, the mean cholo that chases me home all the time."

"The boy with a b-b gun?"

"That's the one."

"Ahhh...yes," he said, rubbing his chin, "I remember him. Where does he live?"

That seemed like a weird question, but I answered it: "Avila? You know where those old boxcars are over by the tracks?"

"Yes."

"In one of those."

"I see ...," he said. "And Tran is the boy from Vietnam?"

"Yeah."

"I suspect that young man has seen things that would make it difficult to intimidate him," Mr. Samuelian says. "Does he also call the Avila boy a cholo as you do?"

That question embarrassed me, and I stammered, "Well...well no. I only call him that because he calls me names too."

"Do I have to ask if you'll take poison because Avila does? Aren't you a little old for me to have to ask you that? Isn't it better when I praise you for achievements? I certainly like that better."

"I guess." I looked down.

He smiled and patted my back. "I thought so. You're growing up, Manuel, and you're a smart boy. Be a leader, not a follower. Don't let your friends influence you to do foolish things. Remember when we talked about 'sticks and stones can break my bones'?"

"Yeah."

"Let's not break anyone's bones with words, or you might end up with an eye-patch like my brother," he winked.

59

That made me laugh a little, at myself really. "Okay," I said. "Avila's just a guy, not a cholo."

Mr. Samuelian was strange. It seemed like he could tell me stuff without sounding like he was being bossy or anything. Most grown-ups were always lecturing kids.

## Chapter 14
# Boys' Hygene

$A$ lecture is what I was expecting that next day at
school because we started this new course all seventh graders had to take. It was taught by Father Mario and it was
called Boys' Hygiene. It only met once a week. The girls
had a separate hygiene class taught by Mrs. Mueller, the
school nurse. All us guys knew what to expect because
the eighth graders had told us that it was really about
S-E-X.

I wanted to be in it, but I was also kind of embarrassed in case we really were going to have to talk to a
priest about that stuff. I was curious, too, though. I knew
from talking to older guys, and even seeing some pictures
that Flaco got from his big brother, Trini, what men and
women had to do to have babies, but I couldn't understand it exactly. The pictures Flaco had made it look awful difficult, almost like fighting. No wonder most people
only did it a few times, like my mother and father with me
their only kid. Flaco said that when you get married you
have to do it once—that's a law—or you'd go to jail or
something. So everybody's mother had tried it, but mothers
hated it. Only fathers liked to do it, he told us.

Flaco he said there were these ladies called "hores"
that did it all the time with lots of guys. He said his big
brother Trini told him there was this one girl at the high

61

school, she was one. Flaco said his brother did it with her. When I even thought about it, my pants bulged; I couldn't help it.

The first day of the course everything was confused since the girls stayed in our regular room, and us guys had to walk to the multi-purpose building, then wait for the teacher. Flaco he'd brought this old, raggedy paperback book he said he got from Trini. "Check it out, ese. Check it out," he urged.

It had these sections underlined, so me and Keeny read them. "Hijole!" he said then gave the book back. I got a lump in my pants reading it.

We didn't notice that Father Mario had come in the back door, but I guess he saw Flaco passing the book around, because he said, "What have you got there, Rójas?"

Flaco turned pale as me. "Ahhh...nothin', Father," he choked, trying to stuff the book into his pocket.

Me and Keeny looked at the floor.

The priest snatched the paperback out of Flaco's hand, glanced at it, then popped Flaco on top of the head with it. "Go to the office!" he ordered. "I'll deal with you later."

Flaco slunk off, his shoulders low as a fish's.

Father Mario didn't even take roll. He stood in front of us and demanded, "How many of you boys read this...this *filth*?" He held the paperback above his head.

I kept looking at the floor, that pleasant lump long gone from my pants.

"Well, if you read this trash, if you excite your bodies, if you spill your seed, you will be abusing part of your body God intends only for the creation of babies by married people!" He sounded real mad.

It was a long, boring class with none of the dirty slides of naked girls the eighth graders said we'd see. In fact, mostly the priest lectured about what he called "the sin of self-abuse."

Afterwards, me, Keeny and Alphabet headed for home. There wasn't any use waiting for Flaco. "You know what that 'sin of self-abuse' means, ese?" Keeny asked.

"Sure," I replied, but I wasn't absolutely certain I did.

Alphabet shook his head. "Don't know," he admitted.

Keeny looked around, then said, "That's playin' with your chorizo, ese."

"Your chorizo?" Tran looked puzzled.

"Your weinie, ese, your weinie," Keeny explained, pointing at his fly, then circling the index finger of one hand with the thumb and index finger of the other, and pumping it real fast.

Alphabet's eyes widened. "Ohhh...," he said.

"And you know what my brother he told me, ese? He said guys that play with themselves they turn to idiots like Robert." Robert was this retarded grown-up that wandered around our neighborhood.

"I heard you can get hair on the palm of your hand, too, ese," I added.

"No lie?" said Keeny, examining one of his palms.

I never told anybody, but I'd stroked myself there a few times when I was in bed. It felt real good. Just the other day, though, I'd forgotten some stuff Abuelita'd asked me to do. I decided not to play with myself anymore.

"It's a mortal sin," said Keeny the expert. "You'll go to hell if you do that."

"What if you think about it?" I asked.

"Mortal sin," said the expert.

"What were you thinking about when you were reading Flaco's book, ese?" I demanded.

"Screw you, pendejo! That doesn't even count anyway," Keeny insisted.

"Oh oh, Keeny," grinned Tran, "maybe go hell."

He didn't tell Tran to screw himself.

A whole week passed and Avila wasn't at school. We all envied him, being suspended I mean. No classes, no homework, no Mr. Mancuso and his wig. It didn't seem fair, though, that he'd be rewarded for getting in trouble by not having to go to school.

Late that week, however, returning home from classes, I was halted by something that chilled my heart. As I passed Mr. Samuelian's yard, I saw in one of the wooden lawn chairs the bronze toad himself, David Avila. I stopped dead in my tracks like one of those animals that freezes so a lion can't see it, but our neighbor had already noticed me. "Manuel!" Mr. Samuelian called. "Please come join us."

Rats! I suspected Avila would be really mad because I'd watched Tran beat him up, so the last thing I needed was to face him now. What could I do, though? I slunk over there as slow as possible, teed-off that Mr. Samuelian would do this to me. "What?" I kind of growled, not looking at Avila.

"David tells me you are the best reader in your class. I want you to help him with this English homework he brought over. He said he would help you learn to improve your Spanish if you did."

I looked up, and the toad nodded at me.

"How come?" I asked. There had to be a trick.

This time Avila averted his eyes. "I can't read...too much," he said.

Mr. Samuelian smiled and patted Avila's broad back. "David's family came from Mexico and he never really got a start in school."

"Yeah," I replied, "well how come he ditches all the time?" That story sounded fishy to me.

"I don' deesh."

"Yeah you do!"

"Tell him what you do, David," urged my neighbor.

Looking embarrassed, Avila said, "I go work weeth

my familia. We peek the cotton last week.'"

"David's not lucky like you and Keeny and Flaco. He has to work to help his family, so he falls behind in school. Then some classmates make fun of him and say he's dumb, call him 'cholo,' so he fights them, right David?"

"Sometimes," Avila nodded, looking embarrassed.

I said, "Oh." I didn't say that stuff as much as some of the other guys did.

"Now," said Mr. Samuelian, rising, "no more time for chat. You take my seat and help David with this English. Help him learn to pronounce some words like 'ditch' and 'little.' You know how you feel when some of your classmates laugh at your version of Spanish, Manuel?"

"Yeah."

"How does that make you feel?"

"Mad."

Mr. Samuelian's caterpillar eyebrows shot up. "So you can understand why David might be angry at some of his classmates."

"Well...I guess."

"You two boys help each other with pronunciations and I'll be back in a second with some lemonade."

So there I was, stuck with the bully. As soon as my neighbor was gone, Avila growled, "How come you call me names?"

"Because you beat me up."

"I beat you up because you call me names," he asserted.

"You started it."

"You and your pendejo friends started eet. You laughed at me. You made fun at me the first day I came to school."

Well, we had done that — I'd almost forgotten — so I backed off. "Well...you dressed funny."

"I don' got no good clothes like you rich pendejos. I only got my old ones from Mexico."

I shook my head. "Hey, we aren't rich, I'm not. Besides, you always call us 'pendejos'."

"What do you call me?" he demanded.

Toad, flashed through my mind, that and cholo. I said, "Nothing."

Thank heavens Mr. Samuelian returned. "Why don't we all just call each other by our names from now on," he suggested. "Let's forget the past and build the future. Manuel, what month is your birthday in?"

"March, why?"

"David, say 'March,' please."

"Marsh."

"You are saying 'Marsh' while Manuel says 'March'. Can you hear the difference?"

Avila shook his head. "What deeference?"

Mr. Samuelian smiled. "No matter," he said. "In English there are two words, 'shill' and 'chill'. Repeat them, please."

"Cheell an' sheell."

"Say them again and try to feel in your mouth the difference in the first sounds."

Avila took a deep breath and said, "Cheell an' sheell." His eyes lit up. "I fill eet! Cheell an' sheell." He grinned like he'd just got a present or something.

Mr. Samuelian grinned too. "Good!" he said. "The lesson has begun."

### Chapter 15
# Mathematics

I was waiting for Flaco and Keeny to show up that morning when Rollo trotted around the corner, sniffing and lifting his leg as he galloped my way. Just then, Tuxedo, Mrs. Alcala's big old tom, he sort of sashayed toward Mr. Samuelian's yard. He didn't seem to notice the dog, but Rollo sure saw him. Zoom! Here he came snarling across the street, his short legs a blur.

Tuxedo, who was as big as the pooch, crouched for a second when he noticed the attack, then he stood and fluffed out. Soon as Rollo got close, the cat not fleeing, I heard this loud "YIP!" All of a sudden, Rollo was chugging in the other direction even faster than he'd come this way, and behind him loped Tuxedo, looking real relaxed but gaining with every stride. Fortunately for the dog, Tuxedo lost interest and slowed, then strolled back to his own yard and flopped onto the dirt like nothing had happened.

I was still laughing when Flaco and Keeny showed up a few minutes later. "Hey, you seen my dog, ese?" asked Flaco. "He got out again."

"He was here, but I think he's gone home."

"Oh. Well it's a good thing he didn't see that old cat. He might've killed it. He hates cats."

We stood there on the dirt border between Mr.

Samuelian's yard and the street, and I guess Flaco was thinking about all the mayhem Rollo might do to poor Tuxedo, then he winked at Keeny and said, "Hey, ese, I think Manuel likes the new girl."

"I do not. I hate her!" I insisted. The new girl was Linda Garcia. She was already the star of the volleyball team, its best hitter and blocker too, but that isn't why I liked her so much. She was real pretty and real smart and she made me feel funny — good funny — when I was around her.

"Simón cabrón," agreed Keeny, giggling. "He gots the hots for her."

"Do not," I snapped.

"Do to," insisted Flaco.

"Do not."

"Then why'd you eat *luuuuunch* with her?" grinned Flaco, stretching the word.

"She was helping me with my Spanish."

"I'll tell you the Spanish she taught him, ese," said Flaco, wrapping his arms around himself, puckered his lips like a whistler and fluttered his eyelids. "Oh, keeess me, Manuel," he said in a high voice, "keeess me, my dahhhling."

"You're so stupid, Flaco, just like your dog."

"Am not, and besides Rollo almost killed a German Shepard the other day!"

"Right," I sneered.

Anyways, I did like Linda, but I wasn't kissing her like dumb Flaco said. "She's just real smart, so she helps me. And you two're pendejos, anyway."

Keeny grinned and said, "The moon was risin' high, ese, and so was Manuel's chor'o."

I almost laughed because that part of what he said was true, but instead I said, "Shut up."

"Oh, keeess me," fluttered Flaco.

"Maybe I'll just *keeess* you with my *feest* Flaco," I warned raising my hands.

"Oh yeah!" He started bouncing.

"Yeah. You gonna sic your dog on me?"

"I could, ese," he said. "He could tear you up." Flaco stood there throwing his hands down, tilting his head, and he swaying like the bad-asses on T.V. I couldn't help grinning because he looked so funny. Just then, Keeny saying, "Hijole! Here comes Avila." Keeny was already jogging away as he spoke.

I gave Flaco one more glare, then called to Keeny. "Hey, wait up, ese! Avila's not gonna punch us out. I told him to meet us here."

Flaco had begun moving too, but he hesitated. "You *told* him?" His tone of voice implied that I'd gone crazy.

"Hey, Keeny!" I yelled. "Come on back!" He didn't, and I saw him disappear like a shadow around the corner. Flaco remained, but kind of hid behind me. "Hi, Avila," I said.

"Hallo, Ryan. You got time to halp me weeth some homework? Meester Mancuso sent eet to my house. Hola Skeenny," he grinned at Flaco. "That your dog I seen it yesterday? It real ugly, like you."

"Skinny," I said to Avila.

"Skiiinny," he repeated.

"Rollo could kill a German Shepard," Flaco meekly protested, looking away from Avila.

"That leetle raton?" Avila guffawed.

"Anyway, my name's not Skinny," Flaco mumbled, but not loud enough to antagonize the big guy.

"Who was that pretty girl I seen you weeth before?" the ex-bully asked me.

"Linda Garcia."

"Leenda ees right. She's real leenda."

"Linda," I said.

"Liiinda," he repeated, grinning.

I noticed that Flaco didn't tease big David about her. In fact, Flaco wasn't saying anything. I'm not even sure he was breathing.

"Boys!" Mr. Samuelian called, and I turned to see him amidst his weeds under his fruit trees. "Come on in and have some lemonade. It's time to help David with his homework."

"Yeah, Skeenny," I said, "let's help David with his homework."

"I gotta go home," said Flaco, still glancing warily at the muscular Avila, and he departed.

Once we were seated under one of Mr. Samuelian's trees, I asked Avila, "What do you have to do?"

"Eet's thees math," his speech was already getting better. He wasn't as dumb as I thought. "I don't get eet," he said.

"Math?" I gulped. "That's not my best subject either. You know who's really good at it, though?"

"Who?" asked Avila.

"Yes, who is, then?" asked my neighbor.

"Alphabet, the new kid."

Mr. Samuelian grinned. "Alphabet?" he said.

"Tran Nguyen, the kid from Vietnam I told you about."

"That Chinaman?" growled Avila, sounding like his old self.

"He's not a Chinaman," I said.

"No," agreed Mr. Samuelian, "he's not. There are no Chinamen here, are there David? And there are no cholos, are there Manuel? We are all neighbors. That is the only label that matters. Can your friend Alphabet come by after school tomorrow? I'd like to meet him and have him help David catch up in math."

"Well...," I was stung by the mention of cholo.

The man turned toward Avila then, and said, "I know

you and the new boy had a fight — Manuel told me. You boys can fight again tomorrow and the day after and the day after, every day forever, and both of you will be no better off. You must learn that your mind is your real weapon, not your fists. If you wish to remain a bully who no one likes, just keep hitting people. You have a fine mind, David. Use it not your fists."

"I got a fine one?"

"You do."

"And you will work with the new boy, won't you?" insisted my neighbor.

"If he don' start nothin' weeth me."

"He didn't start anything the last time," I said.

Before Avila could respond, Mr. Samuelian said, "Last time isn't important. What is important is that there not be a next time."

"Hokay," said Avila. "I weell teach heem the Espanish eef he weell teach me the math...and the keeck fighting."

"Math will be sufficient," said my neighbor. "Now help Manuel with his Spanish, please."

I said nothing, because I agreed that math was enough. Teaching Avila kick fighting would be like sending a bomb to the enemy as far as I was concerned. I wasn't sure he needed it, even if Tran had whipped him.

"You'll ask your new friend, won't you?" Mr. Samuelian urged me.

"I guess."

"And you'll help David with English?"

"Sure."

"And you'll help Manuel with Spanish?"

"Chore," grinned Avila, then he said to me, "Tú hablas español tan peor qué yo hablo el inglés, pendejo."

"No way," I said.

"Algunas maneras, pendejo," he said.

"No way, pendejo."

"Algunas maneras, pendejo." He began grinning.

"No maneras, pendejo!" We both started laughing.

"What is this pendejo word you boys use all the time?" asked Mr. Samuelian.

"It's not really dirty," I said.

"David?" he asked Avila.

The ex-bully shrugged. "Eet just means ... cómo se dice, Ryan?

"It means like a fool or a jerk or a drip. It can be bad if you use it bad or a joke if you joke with it."

"A jerk," said Mr. Samuelian. "Humh," the older man scratched his chin. "And you boys just joke with it?"

"Mostly," I said.

Avila's face turned red. "Help me with this inglés, Ryan," he said quickly.

That night, I had both dreams of my parents, kind of mixed up. I wasn't sure if it was snow or white sand, or if the figure I saw was Momma or Daddy, or maybe la Llorona or Eddie Puss. I only know that I felt real scared or maybe frustrated, like I was caught in something invisible and couldn't escape. I woke up just as I was starting to dribble and was able to get to the bathroom in time.

## Chapter 16
# The Peace Treaty

I telephoned Alphabet that night and asked if he'd consider helping Avila and me with our math (I added myself to sort of soften the proposal). He said yes without me having to talk him into it. I was surprised, but I guess I shouldn't have been. Nothing seemed to scare Tran.

That next day he walked home with Flaco, Keeny and me, joking and playing all the way, but when we turned the corner to my block both Flaco and Keeny quieted. Ahead of us, in front of Mr. Samuelian's house, exactly where Haig Samuelian had once stood and saved me, waited Avila.

"I think I gotta go home, ese," said Keeny.

"Me, too, ese," Flaco agreed. The two tough guys veered away.

"Wait up," I said and they stopped. "It's okay. Avila didn't start anything yesterday." I knew Keeny in particular still couldn't believe my stories about how Avila'd changed. It was hard for me to believe too, but it was real. "Don't be chickens," I shouted.

"Chicken!" challenged Flaco, stopping. "I'm not no chicken."

"Yeah," added Keeny, glancing down the street where

73

the ex-bully stood with fists resting on his hips, "who's a chicken?"

"Then come on," I told them. "Avila's not gonna hurt you."

"We're not ascared of him, ese," asserted Flaco, glancing nervously toward David Avila. "Are we, Keeny?"

"Heck no," Keeny's voice cracked.

"Okay," I said. "Come with us then. Alphabet, let's go help Avila with his homework."

Tran said, "Okay," and we strode toward Mr. Samuelian's yard, those two gallinas clucking along behind.

When we reached Avila, though, I wondered if maybe Keeny and Flaco hadn't been correct. He was scowling and his bronze face was tinged with red. "Hokay," he said directly to Alphabet, "no keecking."

"Kicking," I corrected.

"Kicking," Avila said.

Tran did not back down. "No fighting," he said.

"And no keeck...no kicking," repeated the larger boy.

"Okay," agreed Alphabet. They stood almost chest-to-chest, and I was sure a battle was about to erupt. "And no fighting," Tran repeated.

"Hokay. And no laughing at me."

"Okay. And no calling Chinaman."

"Hokay."

They posed like that for what seemed a long time, long enough for Keeny and Flaco to reluctantly catch up.

"Aren't you boys going to shake hands?" I heard Mr. Samuelian call from his weedy yard. He and his two pals, Jefe and Ramón, had been watching us.

For a moment neither moved. Then Tran extended his right hand and Avila did the same. They clasped and shook them, slowly at first, then faster, and faster, and faster still until both their bodies were jumping and they began laughing.

Mr. Sameulian was laughing too when he said, "Boys! Boys! That's enough. I don't want to have to call an ambulance over the peace treaty. Now come and have some lemonade and we'll do homework."

As we skirted my neighbor's green and towering weeds, Tran stopped and admired them. "This look like my old country," he smiled.

"Well, consider it part of your new home," said Mr. Sameulian. "I understand you're a mathematician, young man."

"It is easy than the English. That one is difficult on me."

"Yes, I understand. My parents came from far away in Armenia and they never fully mastered the language here. But you are young. You will one day speak as badly as these scamps."

"And in the Spanish," added Alphabet.

Avila winked at the others, then said, "Ya lo hablas mejor qué Manuel."

"No way, pendejo," I snapped.

"Oh, Jefe," my neighbor asked the old cowboy, "What does this word, pendejo, mean exactly. These boys use it frequently, but they don't seem to know its precise meaning."

Ramón answered first, "Don't ask that old man. He don't remember nothin'." He had one of those hand-rolled cigarettes in his mouth, and it had been puffed so short that only a smoking ash on his lips showed; it had to be burning him.

Jefe grinned and said, "It is a word used as a mild insult like these boys use it—maybe like ... cómo se dice en el inglés?...like 'jerk' maybe," Jefe said. "What did that Dutchman, the blacksmith, used to call pendejos?...ah, numskulls, verdad?" he asked the other old man.

"Big Henry that worked for Bar K? Yeah, he always

said that word, numskulls," Ramón agreed.

"But if you use it wrong...," Jefe shrugged. "One time this Irish buckaroo named...named?"

"He don't remember nothin', eh Manolito," Ramón winked at me. "Do you mean Juan Terrell that rode for the Circle 7?"

"That's him! Juan Terrell he shot a notch in Paco Cuen's ear because Paco called him that. Remember?"

Ramón nodded. "I remember. Notched him like a calf."

"Shot him?" I gasped.

"They had a shoot-out right in town, wasted a lot of ammunition, but that notch was the only damage. They was both locos, eh Ramón?"

"Crazy as bedbugs," agreed the other vaquero.

"No lie?" said Keeny, tilting his head like a dog hearing a siren, then he whispered to me, "A cowboy shootout in Bakersfield? *Come on...*" Flaco made a face at us that said the same thing.

"She was a rough town in those days," Ramón was saying. "This old man here, he walked right up to them two and took their guns away."

"You took their guns away?" Mr. Samuelian asked.

Jefe shrugged. "They was just gonna hurt somebody."

"He was a rough guy himself, this old man. They didn't wanta tangle too much with him. Besides, he was mayordomo at the ranch."

"Really?" I said.

Keeny whispered to me, "Oh sure, these old guys were tough cowboys. *Sure they were.* No way."

Flaco still had that strange look on his face. He didn't believe them either.

The men didn't seem to notice Keeny and Flaco. "Boys, boys, it's time to start your homework," said Mr. Samuelian. "Don't let these two caballeros distract you. We've got some learning to do here."

Us guys sat at the small wooden table where Mr. Samuelian often wrote in his journal. "Now," he said, "what are we studying in mathematics?"

Flaco groaned, "It's these percentages deals. I don't get it."

"Is easy," said Tran.

"For you, maybe, ese, but not for me," Flaco responded.

"Not for me," admitted David Avila.

Keeny said, "Me either."

I said, "I get it, but it isn't real easy."

"I show you," Alphabet offered, and he took his notebook and pencil from his pack.

"It's too hard," whined Flaco.

Tran shook his head. "Don't be pendejo," he said to the whiner.

We were all laughing when Mr. Samuelian said, "I'll be back with the lemonade in a minute." The three older men left us.

When I went home that afternoon I felt good. Abuelita was resting — it seemed like she rested a lot any more — so I finished an old burrito that I'd left in the refrigerator, then I went into the little room that was mine and for some reason noticed the picture of my father holding me when I was a baby. Abuelita didn't like it very much, but I kept it on the table next to the bed along with one of Mama. Daddy had real long sideburns like a cowboy's in the photograph. He was grinning at me. I looked at it for a long time, wondering what Alaska was like, and when he was coming home, and why he didn't at least write me a letter. I didn't feel all that good anymore.

Finally, I took my piece of blanket from a drawer and held it when I laid down. I didn't cry or anything, I was getting too big for that stuff, but I felt real sad until I fell asleep and had those dreams again.

➤

## Chapter 17
# Tío Tuti

"Hey, Manuel!" my uncle called as he emerged from his big station wagon. My mom's brother, Arturo, was short, like Momma, and round, unlike her. He worked in a real-estate office and wore a necktie all the time. I didn't see him very often because he was busy selling houses and being with his own wife and kids. When he did visit, Aunt Gloria almost never came with him.

"You've grown a foot," he smiled that day. "You're taller than me already. What do you hear from Patrick?"

I lowered my eyes. "I haven't heard from Daddy," I said.

"You haven't? That's weird. Hi, Sarkis!" He waved toward our neighbor, who waved back.

Two of his little kids, my cousins, were with him. They climbed from the car and Justin immediately grasped my hand. "Do you like Rocky and Bullwinkle?" he asked.

I'd hardly ever seen Rocky and Bullwinkle because we didn't get cable T.V., but I said "Yes."

His twin sister Carmen stood back with her chin down and kind of rocked on her heels. "Do you got a girlfriend?" she asked.

My uncle poked me in the ribs, "Do you have a novia?"

I started to say no, but changed my mind. "I like this one girl," I said.

Tuti grinned, but he didn't tease me. "Good for you," he said.

"Is she pretty?" asked Justin.

"Does she got long hair or short hair?" Carmen asked. Before I could answer, I heard Abuelita call from the porch, "O, Arturo y los niños! Come see your Grandmother."

Carmen ran to her, but Justin hesitated. "She's gonna kiss me," he said, then he slowly moved toward Abuelita.

"Muy hombre, that one," said my uncle proudly, then he too walked to embrace his mother.

Later Uncle Tuti piled us into his car and drove us to Taco Bell for lunch. "I want a super burrito and a super nachos and a super tostada and a large coke," demanded Justin.

"You sure you don't want the kitchen sink," chuckled his father.

"I will have one small taco only. No white stuff," my grandmother said. "I don't need much. Just a few visits from my son who's so busy."

Tuti ignored her remark. "Carmen?" he asked.

"Can I have an enchirito and a coke?"

"Sure. Manuel? How about you?"

"Ahhh...how about a chicken fajita and a bean burrito and a root beer."

"What to drink, Mama?"

Grandma waved one hand, and said, "Only coffee, M'ijo."

"Coffee?" said my uncle. "I thought you weren't supposed to drink coffee?"

"Nonsense! I have always drunk coffee."

"I thought Helen told me that the doctor told you..."

"The doctor! Helen is in Los Angeles with Tía Ysabel,

so she doesn't know."

My uncle smiled and said, "All right, Mama, all right. You be the guide."

"Besides," added my grandmother, "I am now drinking the tea that Manuela Aldrette gave to me."

"Manuela the bruja?" he chuckled.

"She is a curandera not a bruja!" Grandma huffed, then she hesitated, narrowed her eyes at him and said, "You are teasing your mother."

"Just kidding, Mom," he grinned, looking a lot like his own little boy.

Justin announced, "I get the prize." A plastic toy was being given with each order.

"Nah uh, I do!" insisted his twin sister.

"I do, dopey!"

"Daddy, Justin called me a name!"

"I'll buy two prizes, don't worry." He drove to the take-out window.

"But he called me a name."

Justin stuck his tongue out at her, then silently mouthed, "Dopey." He turned and grinned at me.

"Daddy!" she called.

"O, pobrecita," soothed her grandmother.

After we ate, Uncle Tuti drove us around town, showing grandma some new houses he would be offering. "When I was a girl, we used to picnic out here," she said. "It was a ranch then."

Later, Abuelita, sighed, then said, "Too bad Gloria couldn't come visit her mother-in-law."

"She has papers to grade, Mama," her son responded. Aunt Gloria taught in a public school, but even I understood why she might stay home. Grandma always ignored Tuti's wife when she did visit, just like she had my father.

Abuelita's eyebrows raised and she asked, "Oh, she's still working then?" My grandma also didn't like women

81

who worked out of their houses.

Uncle Tuti had heard all this before, so he merely smiled, "Just like your daughter, Helen."

"That is different!" snapped Grandma. "Poor Helen has no husband."

"Poor Helen has a husband she chose not to go with," replied Tuti, his voice harder than I was used to hearing from him.

"No! That Irish left her!" Then Grandma jerked her head toward me, and hushed my uncle.

From the back seat, Carmen whined, "Justin touched my prize."

After Uncle Tuti walked his mother back into our little house, and he told the twins to get back into the car to go home, he pulled me aside, and asked, "How's Abuelita been feeling? Has she been dizzy or anything?"

"Dizzy? Maybe once or twice, but not bad."

"Hmmm...okay, Manuel, keep an eye on her and if she gets really dizzy, call me right away, okay?"

"Sure."

Tuti bent and scooped the dirt with one hand like he'd picked something up, then said, "Look what I found. It must be yours." It was a five-dollar bill. He did that almost every time he came to visit, so I only grinned.

"Don't spend it all in one place...unless you spend it on that girlfriend," he winked.

"Thanks Uncle Tuti."

## Chapter 18
# Going to Town

At school that Friday, a bunch of us were shooting baskets during recess when Flaco and Keeny jogged up. They were giggling and panting at the same time. "We just gave fat Anthony a high-riser!" laughed Flaco. "He's after us."

"Yeah, ese," grinned Keeny, "it was a bad wedgie. Bad! While I talked to him, Flaco he snuck up behind Anthony and jerked his chones almost up to his neck. He's real mad, ese."

Flaco was still giggling. "You shoulda seen it, ese! You shoulda seen it! It was so great!"

Anthony earned his nickname — he was a gordo for sure. His trousers seemed to droop all the time, so I knew this story might be true. Flaco and Keeny were always doing stuff like that, but usually only to little kids. In the sixth grade, they'd pantsed this fourth-grader named Raymie Urrea, and tried to hoist his trousers up the flagpole. They didn't even get caught because Raymie was so afraid of them that he didn't tell. But Flaco did get swats from Father Mario the time he snapped Beverly Gonzalez's bra strap—the only bra in the sixth grade. Keeny and him got in dutch for tripping third graders on the way

83

to assembly one day, too, and for throwing green walnuts at some girls from public school that were walking by the playground. Sometimes it seemed like Flaco spent all his time figuring out ways for him and Keeny to get in trouble. Anyways, Flaco was overjoyed that Friday. "Fat Anthony, he never even guessed what we were gonna do," he giggled. "I pulled his underpants clear up his crack. We really tricked him." Then he said, " Oh, oh!"

Fat Anthony Martinez huffed around a corner of the building, his face red, his clothes messed up, and he hollered: "Rójas! Padilla! I'm kickin' your butts!" He could do that, too, if he could ever catch them, but he was real slow. Anyways he ran toward them as fast as he could. The rest of us just stood there and watched while Flaco and Keeny, still chuckling, called, "See you guys," as they jogged away with Anthony in slow-motion pursuit.

Not far behind them, though, real trouble followed: Sister Mary Immaculata. Eventually she rounded everyone up and, when she heard the story, Flaco and Keeny ended up in detention, writing these real long sentences a hundred times each, then picking up trash from the schoolyard.

At least Sister didn't call Flaco and Keeny's mothers, though, so they weren't grounded. We'd planned to go to the matinee the next day at a theater downtown, because we'd all saved up money. We'd have invited Alphabet and Avila too, but we knew Tran had to help his mother work in the little store she operated; Avila hadn't shown up at school on Friday, so I figured he was back in the fields working with his family.

It seemed like most of the kids in town went to the matinee at the California Theater every Saturday. We didn't have money most of the time, but when we did we always joined them and had fun. We'd run into guys we knew from other schools. We'd also see lots of girls we wished we knew.

All week we had to wear blue cords and white shirts to the Catholic school—the required uniform—but on weekends, we got to wear jeans and T-shirts just like public-school kids. The only problem was that the jeans had those shiny buttons, and if you weren't careful one might come undone. "Hey, Manuel," Flaco said that day, "your headlight's showin'."

That meant one of the buttons on my fly was shining, so I reached down and took care of it.

"I think he was playin' with his chor'o, ese," he grinned to Keeny.

"You're the one Father Mario talks about in hygiene class, ese," I replied. "Besides, it makes you deaf to do that."

"Huh?" said Flaco, and we laughed at him.

"Screw you guys!" he snapped, then he changed the subject. "Hey, Manuel, did you see Fat Anthony's face yesterday when we gave him the high riser?" Flaco chuckled as we continued walking, "He was mad, carnal, real mad."

"Yeah, we really jerked his chones. I think they tore, carnal. Grossisimo!"

"Don't let him catch you guys," I warned.

"Ah, he's just a gordo," sneered Flaco.

"Hey, that's what your boy Bernal said that time, but when Anthony got ahold of him, he beat the snot out of him."

"Ese! I could take Anthony easy," bragged Flaco, throwing his hands in his boxer style.

"Me, too, carnal," Keeny said.

"Right," I said. They were both full of it. "What's all this carnal stuff you guys're saying?"

"Hey, ese, if you learn your Spanish, you'll know. Right, Keeny? Besides, it's not for Americans like you, right, Keeny?"

"Simón cabrón." They both laughed.

"Listen, if somebody told you it was cool to call everybody 'dingleberry' you'd do it, carnal." I said that last word the same dopey way they did.

That shut them up for a minute, then Keeny did what those two always did when someone challenged them, he changed the subject. "Hey, carnal," he said to Flaco, "I seen you chewin' on the Host last Sunday at Mass when you took Holy Communion. That's a mortal sin, carnal, chewin' on God."

"You're so full of it," Flaco said. "Besides, I just go to communion so my mother won't ask me all these dumb questions about what sin I did and stuff like that. But if you chew the Host it doesn't even count, carnal. It only counts if you swallow it whole, right, Manuel?"

I shrugged. "I don't know." I didn't remember hearing that theological tidbit in religion class.

"Besides," added Flaco, "Joey Castro and Fat Anthony are gonna die because they stole some Communion wine after they served Mass last Sunday, and they drank it all. Blessed wine turns to a curse when people steal it, carnal, so they get poisoned."

"Does not, pendejo!" snapped Keeny, also an altar boy who I knew had gulped his share of Communion wine.

"Does to, cabrón!"

Even with their arguments, I enjoyed the walk downtown. In fact, I always did. We'd pass this giant, fancy motel and see rich white people being waited on by brown men in white coats, while brown women in white dresses — even one of Keeny's big sisters — cleaned the rooms. Sometimes we'd even make faces at the rich people through the big windows in the restaurant, then run away.

From there, we walked through neighborhoods that had sidewalks and huge, green lawns. None of them had old couches or chickens or rusty cars in the front yards, either, or any kids playing, or even grown-ups out in the yards talking. There weren't any dogs around, except in fenced backyards, anyway. Even Rollo could be king here. It didn't look like a real fun place to live to me, it looked empty, like everybody was hiding inside all the time. But I guess all those people there had lots of money, because the houses were giant, and fancy cars were parked in the driveways. Sometimes we saw brown people mowing lawns there, but all the people we saw who lived in the houses there were white.

We never did anything bad there, like ring doorbells and run, or throw chinaberries at the windows, but sometimes the rich people walked out onto their porches and watched us real close as we passed. That day a mean old lady did that, stood on her porch with her hands on her hips and glared at us, then demanded, "What do you boys want!" We were just strolling by, messing around a little is all, punching shoulders, so I smiled and said, "Nothing." Her face looked real creepy, like a piece of cracked clay.

After we passed, Flaco said, "Hey, Manuel, maybe that lady she was your tía or something. She looked real white just like you. In fact, all those rich gabachos look like you. You must be loaded too."

"Yeah," I said, "I am. I got three and a half dollars. Besides," I added, "you look like the guys working in the yards. Maybe you guys oughta go rake her leaves."

"At least we don't look like a fish's belly like all you gringos," Keeny said.

"At least I don't look like a pendejo like you guys!" I snapped.

"Oh yes you do because you are one!" he responded.

"You are!"

"You are!'

"I know you are, but what am I?"

When we finally arrived downtown, we went to the old Sears store to look at all the people and all the stuff you could buy if you had lots of money. "I'm gonna get me one of those baseball suits," Flaco announced.

"You said that last time, carnal," Keeny laughed.

"Well, I really am, carnal," insisted Flaco. "You just wait."

"We'll wait," I said. I figured we'd have to wait until we had snowy hair like Mr. Samuelian and walked with canes like Mrs. Alcalá before we could ever really afford that kind of stuff. But at least we could look at it.

There was a big drug store called Payless just down the block but we didn't go there anymore, because one time when we were sixth graders Flaco had dared me to steal something. Keeny and him kept it up, saying I was a chicken and stuff, and maybe they wouldn't run around with me any more, so I slipped a plastic whistle into my pocket in there and just walked out. When we'd left the store and were out on the sidewalk. I blew the whistle to show off, but I had this funny half-happy, half-scared feeling. I thought a clerk from the store might sprint up the sidewalk and nab all three of us. I didn't feel safe until we'd finally turned a corner.

"It's great, huh Manuel," urged Flaco. "It feels a lot better than when you buy stuff."

"I guess," was all I said. I had this strange, buzzing feeling I'd never had before.

For a few days, I strutted at school, even bragging a little bit to some others. Then our class had, as usual, been marched from school to the church for Confession before First Friday Mass.

That's when I realized that I had to tell God, or at least Father Mario, what I'd done. Suddenly, I wanted to take the whistle back. We stood in line in the church waiting to enter the dark booth and relieve ourselves of our sins. "Hey, Manuel," grinned Flaco, "you gonna tell?"

"He's gotta," insisted Keeny.

"You boys quiet down!" snapped Sister Mary

Immaculata, and we did till she turned away, then Flaco said, "She's a big black crow," and he flipped her off behind her back.

"Hey, carnal," warned Keeny, "you do that in church and you'll get a curse! Your finger's gonna fall off."

"Won't!" snapped Flaco.

Well, it seemed like Father Mario kept me in the confessional an hour. I changed my voice to this Donald-Duck squeak, but I was sure he knew who it was. "You what?" he said, "and speak up." I told him again. Finally, after a long lecture that I thought everybody in the church could hear, he gave me conditional absolution, telling me I had to return the whistle and to pay for it too. Then he gave me ten Hail Marys, ten Our Fathers, and ten Glory Be's for my penance. Whew! Was I ever glad to get out of there.

In a minute, Keeny knelt next to me. "What'd he tell you, ese?"

"I gotta take that whistle back and pay the lady or else." I felt sick.

"No lie?"

"That's what he said."

The next weekend, all by myself, I had returned to Payless and secretly left the much-used whistle, plus the money for it. Nobody even saw me, but I'd felt like there'd been a spotlight on me the whole time. I hadn't gone back to that store since then, and I'd decided never to let those guys pressure me into doing stuff again. That was dumb...I was.

Sometimes, though, if we had extra money, we'd stop at this drug store across the street from the theater and buy hot dogs and potato chips and root beers. Abuelita never served anything like that at home, and they tasted real good. We didn't have enough this Saturday, though, so we walked directly to the movie theater.

There was a long line of kids waiting to buy tickets because a pirate movie was showing. Flaco and me became pirates ourselves and had a fake sword-fight while we were waiting in line: "On guard!" I called.

"On guard, pendejo! Huh!" he thrust his imaginery sword, but I dodged.

I quickly swung mine—"Ha!"—to cut his head off, but he backed away.

We were still battling, scrambling all over the sidewalk, Keeny laughing at us, when the lady who sold tickets snapped, "Stop that rough-housing, you boys!"

We did immediately because she had once refused admission to a couple of our friends when they played too rough in line. As soon as she turned her attention from us, Flaco said, "She's a pendeja," and he flipped her off. That was his newest tough-guy deal.

"Did you know that you flip off God when you do that?" asked Keeny.

"Huh?"

"What direction does your finger point? At Heaven, carnal." He nodded real slow like he was some kind of priest or something.

"You're so full of it, Keeny," Flaco sneered. "Huh, Ryan?"

I never knew what to think when these guys — or my grandma, for that matter — came up with all their curses and stuff. I thought it was all baloney. They were debating what would happen to Flaco's middle finger when the line finally began to move.

90

## Chapter 19
# Matinee

I kind of hoped Linda, the new girl in our class, would be at the theater that day, but I didn't tell Flaco or Keeny that. I'd heard her tell another girl that she might attend the show Saturday. She wasn't there, though, or at least I didn't see her.

A double feature was playing and the first movie was a dopey love story, all smooching and stuff, those long, long movie kisses. Us guys we sat in the balcony and teased these two girls that Keeny knew from Lincoln School, then we pooled our money to buy a box of popcorn. Keeny said Flaco was eating too much and Flaco said he wasn't and the usher said for us to quiet down. While those two argued in hissed whispers — "You are too, pendejo." "I am not, pendejo." — I ate most of the popcorn.

Before the dumb love movie finally ended, Flaco began scraping dry wads of chewing gum from underneath seats and throwing them over the balcony. He always did that, but I told him to stop. I didn't want to get kicked out after paying my money.

I decided to go to the rest-room. If I waited until intermission, that place would be so crowded that somebody might pee on my shoes like happened to me once before. The boys' bathroom was in the upstairs lobby behind the balcony, and I walked past these three big guys as I went in it. I felt them look at me, but they didn't say anything so I just forgot about it.

When I came out, the same three were still there but this time one of them said, "Hey, guy," and sort of slouched directly in front of me, his big chest bumping me. He was husky, in high school for sure, and he held a cigarette in one hand. "You, like, wanna puff?" he asked with this real strange smile on his face, like a groggy lizard.

"I don't smoke," I said.

"Like, what's wrong, guy? Chicken?"

"I just don't." The other two joined him and they blocked my way back to the balcony. No one else was in the upstairs lobby.

"You look just like the guy I like seen sittin' with two little greasers. Do you, like, run around with greasy Mex'cans?"

I sensed that I couldn't say anything to satisfy him, so I said nothing.

He rolled his shoulder toward me, and I was jolted as he slapped my face. "Like, answer me you little Mex'can-lover," he growled. "Do you?"

All three of them were older and bigger than me, and I knew I couldn't get away. Before I could think of a reply, one of the others said, "I bet other white kids won't even run around with this little queer, that's why he has to run around with spics."

"Kiss off, pendejo," I told him. They might beat me up, but I wasn't going to say what they wanted me to.

"He, like, even talks Mex'can," spat the biggest one, then he slapped me again, and said real fast to his pals, "Like, watch out for the usher while I punch this little faggot out."

92

I backed away, but he followed me with his large right fist cocked.

That's when I heard a familiar voice—"Pendejos!"—and David Avila charged into the lobby from downstairs at a run, smacking the guy who was after me so hard that the white aggressor tumbled onto the worn carpet, one cheek suddenly looking like a plumb. David kicked him once, twice. The other two were surprised and at first they just kind of fluttered there and said, "Hey!" Avila, seeing that the first guy wouldn't getting up real soon, went after them and they ran. He chased them down the stairs, and I heard one of the bullies yelling, "We never did nothin'!"

An usher immediately appeared and demanded, "What's going on? Who's been smoking?"

It had all happened so fast that, at first, I didn't know what to say. Finally, I told him, "That guy there started a fight with another guy and he got beat up. The other guy he took off." I didn't mention that the other guy —Avila — took off chasing two bullies.

"Are you sure it wasn't you?" By now lots of kids — including Flaco and Keeny — had evacuated the balcony to see what the commotion was and they hovered all around. "No, I guess not," the usher answered his own question. "You're too small. And you say this clown started it?"

"Yeah. And he was smoking, too."

He turned then toward the tough guy, who had risen unsteadily holding his swollen cheek. "Come on, mister," the usher ordered, and he grasped one of older boy's arms and marched him down the stairs.

"What happened, ese?" Keeny asked.

"Yeah, carnal, what happened?" Flaco joined in.

"I don't know for sure, but that guy and two others were gonna beat me up, and Avila showed up. He knocked that one guy on his keister and chased the other ones."

Keeny looked excited. "No lie?" he said. "Avila did that?"

"On his what?" asked Flaco.

"His keister. My dad used to say that."

"What's a keister?"

I shrugged. "I don't know for sure. Who cares, anyways?"

"Tell us what Avila did, ese," Keeny insisted.

"He knocked that guy on his ass is what! The other ones took off running."

"How come they were gonna beat you up, ese? Did you call 'em a name?"

"No, I never did anything." I really didn't know why. "They just wanted to beat me up, I guess. They said they didn't like Mexicans."

"You're not a Mexican," said Flaco.

Keeny disagreed. "He is too."

"He is not, pendejo."

"Is too, pendejo, or how come those white guys were gonna beat him up?"

I just knew I was Manuel and it didn't matter if I was Mexican or Irish or what, I didn't want high-school guys beating me up. And I was sure going to thank Avila, that much was sure. "Come on, you guys," I said. "We're gonna miss the pirate movie."

# Chapter 20
# Abuelita's Lesson

I brought that form home from school again, along with a fresh copy to fill out. "Mr. Mancuso, the teacher, he gave this back to me, Abuelita. He says we have to fill out the new one properly."

"What form is that, mi'jito?"

"That one about what I am ... you know ... what kind of boy I am. 'White/Euro-American, Native American, Asian, Black/Afro-American, Middle-Eastern, Pacific Islander, Mexican-American /Chicano, Other Hispanic.' That stuff."

"I told you before, you are Spanish like your Grandmother."

"Okay," I said. "Please sign this for me." I handed her the form and she asked, "Where?" so I pointed to the line. After she finished, I placed a check in the box for "Pacific Islander." The whole thing seemed dumb to me.

It was warm that evening, so Abuelita and me wandered outside where there was a light breeze. We sat on the old couch in front of our little house, and those dumb chickens that never seemed to learn my grandma was a neck-wringer crowded around us hoping for garbage. "Ah," she said, "it smells so nice out here, doesn't it

95

mi'jito."

"Yeah," I said. "I think all those big plants of Mr. Samuelian's do that...smell so good I mean."

She snorted, "His weeds!"

"What'd you get in the mail today, Abuelita? I saw you take a letter into your room."

She'd looked the way I'd felt when I was stealing that whistle, and she said, "Just something private, mi'jito. Do not worry about it."

Then I remembered what I'd been meaning to ask her. "Abuelita, did you ever hear of a guy named Eddie Puss or a lady named la Llorona?"

She immediately made the sign of the cross, and said, "I do not know that Eddie, but I have with these eyes seen the evil la Llorona on the plains of Rancho San Emedio. Cross yourself, mi'jito. If you even talk of her, cross yourself because she is cursed."

I obeyed.

"How come she's cursed, though?"

"Oh, mi'jito, that is a terrible story..."

She didn't finish because just then something flew over us in the dark, a big white bird it looked like. "Look Abuelita," I said, pointing at it, "an owl, or a hawk, maybe."

"¡Madre de Dios!," said my grandmother, and she made the sign of the Cross again, three times. "Cross yourself, mi'jito! Cross yourself right now!"

She sounded so scared that I crossed myself again.

"In the night, m'ijo," Abuelita told me, "los Chisos flies in search of souls."

Sometimes it seemed like there were so many ghosts and stuff around our neighborhood that there shouldn't be any souls left.

Anyways, that was the first time I'd ever seen a big bird like that. "What's los Chisos mean, Abuelita?"

"Ohhhh," her voice quivered, "evil spirits that fly in

the night in the shape of birds, and steal the souls of sinners. They are muy peligroso, mi'jito. Muy peligroso."

"Really?" I wondered what would happen if it flew over the rowdy Flaco's yard.

"Atheists like that Armenian had better beware!" she warned.

Sometimes she even used English words I didn't understand. "What's an atheist?"

"Those are the evil ones who do not believe in God, my son."

I thought about that, then said, "But Mr. Samuelian believes in God. He talks about God all the time."

This time she paused, then explained, "Then why do I never see him at the one true church where we go. Beware of him, mi'jito, and his weeds. God doesn't want them to grow."

"How come they grow then, his weeds I mean?"

She looked startled and her mouth moved without sound for a second. Finally she said, "The Evil One, mi'jito. The Evil One has many powers."

"Like growing weeds?" She had to be kidding.

"Of course. Flowers are God's plants. Weeds are the devil's."

When I realized that she was serious, I started to protest, but the telephone rang in our house, and I said, "The phone."

"Oh?" she responded. Abuelita didn't hear real good. "I wonder who that is. You get it mi'jito, I will be right in."

I sprinted into the house and answered it. "Hi honey," my mom said, "How are you? How's school? Are you doing good?"

"I'm fine Mom and guess what? Did I tell you that we got these excellent computers at school and you can draw pictures with them or write essays or figure out math. Mom...?"

"What honey?"

"Do you think we could ever buy one, a computer I mean?"

"Buy a computer? No, I don't think so. Not right now, anyway. We really don't have that kind of money.

"Oh," I said. I'd expected that she'd say we couldn't afford a computer, but what the heck, it was worth a try.

"Mom, guess what else. Me and Keeny and Flaco we're helping this kid named David Avila to catch up in school. And this other kid named Tran, he's helping us with math — we're gonna start some algebra stuff pretty soon. And..."

"Slow down, m'ijo, slow down," she urged, chuckling. "Have you heard from Daddy?"

"Not since that card and present last Christmas."

"That's so strange. I just had a note from him, and I got the impression he'd written to you. Well, I'll be coming up for a visit next weekend and we'll talk about it then. I've got two days off. We'll go out to the park and maybe we can take your friends. Has Grandma been okay? Has she been dizzy or anything?

"She's okay. Can I ask you a question?"

"Of course."

"Why does Grandma always call people by those names or nationalities or whatever, like Armenian or Portugee or colored or ... or Irish?"

I heard my mother sigh before she said, "Well, that's a long, long story, and I don't know all of it. When Abuelita was growing up around here she suffered a lot of abuse because she was a Mexican, and it just affected her that way. She can't seem to get those things out of her mind now, and she uses those words to explain..." her voice trailed away like she couldn't find the right words.

"I really don't know," she finally admitted. After another pause, she asked, "Do you know what 'racism' means,

Manuel?"

"Not liking colored people?"

"Not liking any people usually because they're a different color, like white people not liking black people, or black people not liking brown people, or brown people not liking yellow people just because they're different. When that starts, it seems like all it does is create more racism. Don't let that happen to you, honey. Trust me, life's hard enough without that craziness. Just judge people by how they act, not what color they are, okay?" She sounded real serious.

"Okay, Mom." I really meant it too. "Does Grandma have that 'racism' stuff?"

She said only, "Can I talk with her for a moment?"

"Sure," I replied. I needed to think about what she'd told me.

"I love you, honey, and I miss you," Momma said.

"Me too, Momma." My eyes got all warm like they were melting or something. I wanted her to move back with us. And I wanted my father to come home too. I called Abuelita then.

When she finally hung up, I asked my grandmother what they'd been talking about. "Oh nothing you'd understand, mi'jito, grown-up talk. What is that book you brought home? It is from the library?"

"It's a book about dinosaurs that Mr. Samuelian lent me."

She wrinkled her nose like she smelled something bad. "Oh, that Armenian. What kind of a book did you say?"

"About prehistoric dinosaurs."

"Those big lizards? Do you believe in them?"

Believe in them? I grinned. "Sure." I opened the volume and displayed a full-page drawing of a stegosaurus.

"Where do they live?"

I really thought she was kidding, but I said, "They

don't live, Abuelita. They're what you call extinct, all dead."

"They are? Well, when did they live?"

"I don't know, about a jillion years ago, I guess."

"Ah!" She stood and chuckled. "How could they be real if God did not create them in the Garden and Noah did not carry them in the Ark? Are they mentioned in the Bible? Are they? You have been fooled, mi'jito."

"But they were real, honest."

"Have you ever seen one?" she demanded.

"Of course not."

"Yes," she said, and nodded her chin just like that settled everything.

Well, it stumped me for a minute, then I asked, "Have you ever seen God?"

"What a thing to ask your grandmother!"

"Have you, though?"

"I have seen many things, mi'jito. Many, many things you cannot understand."

"But if you haven't..."

"This is how you act after you talk to that Armenian?"

I wasn't letting go. "Besides we study dinosaurs at Catholic school," I told her.

"The nuns teach such things?" Her whole face shifted upward up like an exclamation mark.

"Mr. Mancuso's my teacher this year, you know that."

"Of course, a man and not even a priest. The nuns would never teach such nonsense." She reached over and closed the book I held. "The Holy Bible is the only book you need, mi'jito. I will talk to the nuns about that Mr. Mancuso and his dinosaurs."

## Chapter 21
# Robert and Linda

Horsing around on the way home from school the following Tuesday, Flaco, Keeny and me saw Robert, that retarded grown-up guy. My mind was drifting toward Linda Garcia, who lived not too far from Keeny, so I didn't pay much attention when Flaco grinned and said, "Hey, ese, let's go mess with the loco, want to?"

Keeny grinned, "Simón cabrón!"

"Not me," I told them.

"What're you, ese, chicken?" sneered Flaco.

"No, I'm just not dumb enough to do all the stuff you do, pendejo."

Robert he lived near Keeny's house, and he always pulled a wagon around the neighborhood looking for good junk. I know that Mr. Samuelian sometimes gave him bags of fruit, old clothes, aluminum cans, things like that. Robert's face was real smooth, like it didn't have any bones under it, and his eyes were little. He wore this dirty old baseball cap and, two or three shirts at a time. He talked funny, too, like his nose was plugged up.

Anyways, some dumb guys used to tease him. One day I saw Flaco put his hand out and say, "Hey, Robert! Wanta be friends?" When Robert grinned and stuck his hand out, Flaco pulled his back real fast with his thumb stuck out like he was hitch-hiking, and said, "Up the river!" We'd all laughed, but Robert didn't. He looked like he might cry, and I was sorry that Flaco'd done that.

Other times when we'd see the simple-minded guy, Keeny or Flaco might call "Hey Robert! Hey loco! Can't catch us!" He'd sometimes take off and run after them, but they'd get away. One time, though, when Flaco had this bicycle his mother'd bought at the police auction, he was teasing Robert, but he got tangled up in his bike. By the time he got it straightened out, Robert was almost on him, so Flaco dropped the bike and ran.

Robert took the bicycle away. Us kids all knew he was strong as Frankenstein, so none of us dared to try and grab the it back from him. Flaco was real scared, and he hustled home and told what happened, but not the whole truth. His mother got his bike back for him.

"You gonna tell your momma again if he gets your bike, chicken," I said to Flaco.

"You're the chicken, chicken," he insisted, throwing down his hands in his tough guy act, but staying far away from me.

"Yeah, well I'm not chicken enough to go along with you, and don't call me that again or I'll make you take it back."

"Okay, Ryan," he said to me, still, sort of behind Keeny. "You're no fun anyway."

So those two swaggered over toward Robert, big buddies, but the older man he kept shuffling along like he didn't even notice them. Pretty soon Flaco charged over to Robert, waved his arms, and yelled something. Robert dropped the handle of his wagon and began chasing Flaco, but when he did, Keeny darted over and grabbed the wagon and began pulling it in the opposite direction. It was full of old newspapers and other junk that began to fall out of it as

Keeny bumped over rocks and pot-holes.

Robert stopped, looked back, and saw his wagon disappearing. Instead of running after Keeny, he started crying. I felt bad to see a poor retarded guy losing all the stuff he'd collected and to see him crying like a little kid, so I yelled at Keeny: "Hey! That's enough! Come on! Bring it back to him, pendejo!"

Grinning like a jack-o-lantern, he ignored me, so I took off after him. I was going to make him return that wagon. "Hey, Keeny! You'd better come back!"

Just before the thief reached the corner, though, a big lady in a mu-mu came out of a house and stationed herself in front of him. I stopped chasing him because I knew he was in deep trouble. She was another of his aunts, Tía Beatriz. He noticed her too late, and slowed just as he reached her. While the weeping Robert was shuffling toward them, she slapped Keeny's face — Pop! — right in front of everyone. "You little fool. You wait until I tell your mother what you done. How's that poor man gonna live? You got life too easy with your school books and clean clothes!" She was shaking him like a dry mop. "Don't let me ever catch you botherin' him no more. You hear?" She shook him harder, then slapped him again: Pop!

Keeny mumbled something, and she let him go. Then she ordered him to pick up Robert's stuff, and the red-faced boy began to do that right away.

Then Tía Beatriz noticed me across the street, and she demanded, "Were you helping this malcriado, Manuel Ryan?"

"No," I said. "But I'll help pick up Robert's stuff."

A minute later I was tossing old rags and cans and papers into the wagon, and I whispered to Keeny, "Aren't you glad you listened to Flaco?"

"Shut up!" he snapped, a red hand-print still clear on his face.

"Hey, don't be mad at me, ese," I couldn't help grinning. "Flaco's the one that got you in trouble, and he's not even helping you."

He glanced at me for a second like he hadn't thought of that, then said, "I'm gonna beat up that cabrón tomorrow."

"Snap it up there, you two," ordered Tía Beatriz, and we did. Boy, was I glad I hadn't teased Robert.

That evening, while my grandmother watched the television that Uncle Tuti'd given her for Christmas, I snuck into the kitchen and gazed at the telephone. I had talked with Linda Garcia for a little while during lunch hour at school. Not for very long, though, because I didn't want Flaco and Keeny to see me. The last thing Linda had said to me was, "Why don't you call me up tonight so we can talk some more." Then she'd given me her number.

I really liked her. I felt good just being around her, but sometimes I got these dirty feelings too, the kind that Father Mario said we weren't supposed to have. I couldn't seem to help myself, though, and my pants would all of a sudden feel too tight. Father Mario had warned us about that — "filthy thoughts" — in Boys' Hygiene class too. I really didn't want to think dirty stuff about Linda because I liked her. It made me feel guilty when I did because she was special.

I'd never even telephoned a girl before, but I wanted to call Linda. The trouble was, I didn't know what to say, so I sat there dreaming about our conversation: "Hello, Manuel. I'm so happy you called. You're the only boy in the world I want to talk to, and when we grow up I want to marry you." No, she wouldn't say that.

"Hello, Manuel. I wanted you to call me because you're so cute and nice." No, not that either.

"Hello, Manuel, you dope. Hah hah! I was just fooling when I told you to call me. I don't even like you. You're all pale and white like a dead fish. I just wanted to

104

tell the other girls you called so we could make fun of you." That was more like it.

I continued sitting there staring at the old black telephone with its round dial. Oh, heck. I got up and found my book bag, then carried it into the kitchen so I could begin my homework, glancing over at the telephone every once in awhile.

I finished my English and history, then delayed starting on math, my worst subject. I thought maybe I should call Alphabet to help me, and that made me think about telephoning Linda, and that tightened my pants, so I forced her out of my mind and thought of my father; I should telephone him. I'd long ago asked my grandmother if she had a number for him, and she'd snorted no. This time, afer checking to make sure Abuelita was still watching television, I picked up the telephone book and looked up "Out-of-Area Directory Assistance": 1-area code-555-1212. Next I looked up the area code for Alaska: 907.

I sat there for what seemed like a long time, my breath quicker than before and feeling sneaky. After looking around as though people might be watching me, I dialed 1-907-555-1212.

After one ring, a voice that sounded like a lady talking through a pipe said, "What city please?"

My breath grew quicker. I didn't know what city. I just knew Alaska.

"What city please?" that voice repeated.

I could think of nothing else to say, so I snapped, "Wrong number!" and slammed the receiver down.

For a second I closed my eyes, embarrassed and vaguely scared, then the phone rang, and I was sure it was that lady tracking me down, and that she was going to tell my grandmother — maybe even the cops.

My hand hovered over the receiver, but hesitated. I let it sound one more time, took a deep breath, then lifted the receiver and said in a froggy little voice the lady wouldn't recognize, "Hello."

"Hello, this is Linda Garcia. Is Manuel Ryan there?"

"Oh," I said, "hi."

"Manuel? You sounded funny."

"I was clearing my throat."

"I was afraid you'd forgotten to call me," she said.

"You were?"

"Yes. You didn't, did you?"

"No, I was just gonna call. I had to finish my homework first."

"Me, too," she giggled and it wasn't the "Hah hah!" I'd feared, but a happy tinkling. It sounded so cool!

A half-hour later, I had just hung up and my face was covered with a big smile, when I heard, "Who were you talking to, mi'jito?"

Abuelita stood in the doorway. My grandmother amazed me. She was kind of deaf, but it seemed like she always heard stuff I didn't want her to.

"Oh...," I stammered, "a kid from school."

"Oh," she said, "what is his name?"

"Garcia. I've gotta call Tran so I can finish my math."

"Garcia...?" she said. "I hope it isn't one of those black Cubans that have moved into the parish.

Well, Linda's family wasn't from Cuba, and she sure wasn't black. She was kind of cinnamon color, the prettiest skin I'd ever seen. I really didn't like the way this conversation was going, so before Abuelita could say more, I dialed Alphabet and said "Hello" even though no one answered. My grandma stood silently for a moment longer, then returned to her television show.

106

## Chapter 22
# The Girlfriend

I couldn't wait to get to school that next morning so I could talk to Linda. I hustled out the door with my book bag unzipped and my shirt half-tucked in, then I heard Abuelita call: "Manuel! Mi'jito! You forgot your lunch!"

When I hurried back to pick up the bag containing a burrito and an apple, Grandma asked, "What's the hurry? Are you and those malcriados up to something?" She arched her eyebrows in accusation.

"No, we're just gonna play basketball is all."

"Well, all right. Be careful, mi'jito."

I walked nice and slow to the corner because I figured she was watching me, but once I was out of sight, I took off at a run. Just before I arrived at school, I slowed down, tucked my shirt back in, and carefully arranged my hair with the new comb I'd bought. Then I strolled as casually as I could toward the basketball courts.

Alphabet was already shooting buckets, and he waved me over. I scanned the yard but didn't see Linda. Well, I was real early, so I joined Tran and took a few shots myself—he was helping me learn a jump-hook. A few minutes later, David Avila lumbered up and joined us. He couldn't play basketball very good, but he tried lots of goofy stuff: between-the-legs shots, behind-the-back shots, half-court shots. I think he did that because he had trouble even making lay-ins and free throws, so he figured if he was going to miss anyway, he might as well miss fancy ones. I don't think he ever got to play basketball before he enrolled at Guadalupe.

I was wearing my Timex watch, and I kept checking it: 7:45 the first time, then 7:49, then 7:50. Classes started at 8:45. I kept shooting baskets, kidding with Alphabet and Avila, but my eyes were scanning the school yard.

"Hey, Ryan, you missed everything!" laughed Avila, who was an expert on air balls.

Then I noticed Linda round a corner with two other girls. They all carried binders across their chests, and they were gabbing. They sat on a bench against a wall near the basketball court and continued talking. Linda smiled at me, and I managed to sink a hook shot for her. But those other two girls stayed with her, so I kept shooting baskets.

"Míra," Avila said to me when he noticed Linda, "su novia." He and Alphabet laughed and pushed me lightly toward her.

Just then Linda stood and walked toward us, and my breath caught. "Hi, Manuel," she smiled. "Hi David. Hi Tran." Then she turned her attention to me. "I thought you were going to talk to me this morning?"

"You had friends..."

"I was waiting for you."

"You were? Well...ah...let's talk." I felt funny. "See you guys," I said to my basketball buddies, feeling real proud.

We walked to the bench and sat together. "It was neat when we talked on the phone last night," she said.

"I thought it was cool."

"Do you like Carmen that's in our class?" she asked.

I thought a second. "Carmen? I don't know."

"Sometimes I like her," she said. "Sometimes I don't...when she says mean things."

This was new to me. I had no idea what Carmen ever said. "Oh, yeah?"

"But sometimes she's nice."

"Oh." I wanted to be near Linda, but I couldn't think of anything to say.

"You made a good shot," she smiled.

"Thanks. Tran's the best though."

"And David's the worst, huh?"

I grinned. "Yeah, but he's a good guy."

"He used to be mean."

"It wasn't his fault. He's a good guy now."

"And he's doing better in class, too, isn't he?"

"Yeah. We study together sometimes, him and Tran and me."

"Are you going out for basketball? I'll be playing on the girls team."

"Really? What position?"

"Forward, I think, because I can jump. We don't have any really tall girls this year. How about you?"

"Father Mario says he'll put me at forward," I said.

"Maybe we can practice shooting together some time."

"Sure," I said, but I wasn't sure I wanted the guys seeing me playing basketball with a girl.

"What're you doing for your science project?" she asked.

"Ah...dinosaurs, I think," I replied.

"Oh, really!" Linda smiled. "Can I be your partner?"

Surprised by her question, I stammered, "Sure. That'd be awesome. We can go to the library together."

Just then Keeny and Flaco strode into the school yard separately. Their clothes were all messed up and dusty, their faces had some red marks and their hair was messed up too. They didn't look at each other, but both of them headed for the basketball court. I knew what had to have happened. I hoped they'd both lost the fight.

After school that day, I walked Linda home. We talked about lots of stuff — when we were little, the schools we'd attended before Guadalupe, and I told her what had happened the day before with Robert. Finally I asked, "Do you speak Spanish?"

"Yes, but not too good," she smiled. "I understand good, though. How about you?"

"I'm just learning. I didn't hear much Spanish until I moved in with my abuela."

"Where's your mom and dad?" Linda asked.

"Oh...," I hesitated, "he had to go to Alaska for a job, and she's in L.A."

"Are they divorced? That's a sin." We'd heard about divorce in our religion classes.

"I don't think they are, but they aren't together."

"Alaska is neat. That's where there's polar bears."

"I want to go up there with my dad some day."

Linda stopped and touched my forearm. "I'd miss you if you did, Manuel."

It was like in a movie. My heart got real warm and my pants got real tight. We were outside her house — it was bigger than ours, a lot bigger and painted real nice. It had a sidewalk in front, too, and a lawn. Linda looked at me kind of strangely, then smiled and said, "Manuel, can I ask you a question?"

"Sure."

"Are you poor? Carmen says you are and that I shouldn't be your friend."

"Poor? Me? Heck no." I said that, but the question made me think. How could we be? Abuelita and me had our house and food and clothes. "I don't think so, anyways," I added.

"Well, I don't care if you are. I like you better than Carmen and her friends."

"Great. I like you too. A lot." I kind of choked on those last words. It's hard to say that kind of stuff to a girl. I promised to telephone her that night, then I walked home so high that my feet didn't touch ground. But I did notice that only a couple of blocks from where she lived, closer to our house, there were no sidewalks, and pretty soon the streets had big holes in them, and there was no grass but lots of old cars and even garbage in the yards. Maybe we *were* poor.

To me, our area didn't look poor exactly, but kind of messy and interesting. I didn't see any people who looked skinny as straws like on the TV news. I didn't see any beggars. When the big farms around Bakersfield were harvesting, almost everybody disappeared during the day, but during winter there were lots of people, even grown men, just sitting around. I guess I really didn't know what "poor" meant. I sure didn't feel poor. Right then, in fact, I felt great.

I decided to ask Mr. Samuelian.

When I turned the corner and walked past our neighbor's yard, I heard voices among the weeds and trees. "Would you rather be chickens or fools?" Mr. Samuelian quietly demanded of Flaco and Keeny, who sat looking at the ground. "You both acted like fools when you attacked that poor, handicapped man. Perhaps Beatriz is right, you boys have had life too easy." Mr. Samuelian noticed me and said, "Ah, Manuel, come join us. We're discussing pranks and respect for the feelings of others."

Flaco made a face when my neighbor wasn't looking.

"I understand that you and Keeny and Flaco were harassing Robert the other day. Is this true?"

"Me and Keeny and Flaco! No, it's not true. Who said I was?" I glared at my so-called friends.

111

Flaco looked down and admitted, "He never."

"Ah, so the story changes. But you were there?"

"Yeah," I said, "but I didn't do it."

"You didn't stop Keeny and Flaco, though, did you?"

"No. Not at first, anyways."

"Well, I believe you. You boys should be helping Robert the way the rest of us do. You should thank God that you are healthy and have warm homes. You must understand that we really *are* our brothers' keepers. People like Robert can't help themselves, so we must help them. You may not be able to imagine it, but you too may one day be sick or old or hungry. Treat Robert the way you'd want to be treated. He can't help his condition, but we can help our behavior, can't we?"

We all nodded. He was talking to us like we were little kids, but I understood why.

"And you two had a fight?" he asked Keeny and Flaco.

Keeny said, "He started it."

"No, you hit me first."

"Because you got me in dutch, pendejo."

"Hold on! Hold on! Do you see how evil breeds evil? First you harass a poor, helpless man, and now you're fighting each other. The answer is to think before you act. Treat others as you'd like to be treated. You must act responsibly." He didn't yell, but he sounded pretty mad to me.

Boy! Was I ever glad that I hadn't teased Robert.

## Chapter 23
# Storytellers

Keeny and Flaco avoided Mr. Samuelian for a few days after he chewed them out. I started walking Linda home from school every afternoon, and sometimes we touched hands. When that did happen, it felt like the warmest, nicest electricity in the world — Zappo! I always remembered that question about whether I was poor when I got to her neighborhood with its new cars and lawns and sidewalks, but I usually forgot it by the time I got back to my house.

Late that next week, though, I spied Mr. Samuelian at the front of his lot holding a hoe and gazing toward the street as I wandered back from Linda's house, so I waved then approached him, and said, "Can I ask you a question?"

"You know you can, but when you start like that, I know it's serious. Come sit down and tell me what's on your mind."

"Well," I said, after plopping into one of the wooden yard chairs, trying to say it just the right way, "what makes people poor?"

"What makes people poor? Do you mean what creates poverty?"

Creates poverty? I wasn't even sure what that meant. "No, I don't think that's what I mean. I mean how can you tell if you're poor or not?"

"Ah, and why do you ask?"

"Oh, some kids at school think I'm poor."

His eyebrows seemed to quiver, then he said, "They do? Well, you're not. They're probably confusing a lack of money or a lack of possessions with being poor. I have very little money, but I have a small pension, enough to eat, a place to live, and wonderful friends and family. Am I poor? Of course not."

"But you don't have a fancy car or a big house or..."

He grinned. "I don't drive. I am a small man with a small house. I had a wonderful wife whom I miss every day, but at least we had forty-one years together. I have a brother, cousins and a family. I am content.

"But there are too many people with no house, no food, no friends: they are poor and we should pray for them. There are also people with big houses and fancy cars and lots of money, but nobody loves them: they are poor too, and they deserve our prayers."

"Boy," I said, "things're sure complicated."

"Yes," he said, they are. "Here come two rich men, wealthy with friends and memories."

The rattletrap pickup Jefe and Ramón traveled in pulled up in front of the yard, and from it climbed the two old cowboys. They shuffled up and nodded, "Hola, Sarkis. Hola, Manolito," said Jefe.

"¿Que tal?" smiled Ramón.

They sat and Mr. Samuelian walked into his house, saying, "I must prepare coffee for these two. They only come by to drain my cups."

"That is true, Manolito," winked Ramón. "Free coffee."

Jefe added. "And for the free fruit, too, of course."

After Mr. Samuelian went into his house to prepare

coffee, Ramón asked, "Who owns that ugly little dog?"

Rollo was trotting by, stopping to lift his leg on one of the pickup's tires. "That's Flaco's," I said. "He told me it killed a cat yesterday."

"Must've been a small cat," grunted Jefe.

Ramón was shaking his head. "That's sure an ugly dog," he chuckled. "He looks like the north end of a horse goin' south." Then he added, pointing at Tuxedo "Look at the size of that black and white gato over there. Looks like a panther"

"Can't be," chuckled Ramón, "it's too big."

We all laughed again.

Once the coffee was served and everyone settled into conversation, they didn't act like they wanted me to leave the way grownups usually do to kids. "Was my abuelo really a good cowboy?" I asked.

"Manolo? Oh yeah, he was a good one, eh Ramón?"

The other vaquero nodded. "Back in those days, if you weren't good the mayordomo he'd run you off in no time. Nobody ever run Manolo Higuera off. In fact, I remember that guy he was boss at Circle-Bar-Z...what's his name?..."

"Aguilar, Teresino Aguilar, hombre. He don't remember nothin', that old timer," Jefe said to us.

"...Teresino Aguilar tried to get Manolo to quit and go to work for him, but Manolo he was loyal too. He stayed with us."

"That Aguilar, he used to ride a mule instead of a horse, remember?"

"Oh, yeah, and that tough guy from Texas he laughed at him in the rodeo parade at San Luis Obispo, so Aguilar he roped that guy and put him in a water trough."

"He laughed at the wrong guy."

"I should say so," smiled Mr. Samuelian.

Well, that was just the beginning of the stories. I stayed

until almost dark listening to them. "To a true vaquero, like this boy's abuelo," Jefe asserted, "a horse was like what you call it a book...a open book...to show if the rider was a caballero or a pendejo. If a caballero rode it, a horse was always calm, because caballeros never fight with their horses. But if the rider was a pendejo, it would be mean and nervous because pendejos always act like...well, like pendejos. They fight their horses."

"Is that right?" said my neighbor. "Have an apple, Manuel."

"Thanks."

Jefe kept right on talking. "Oh yeah. Just ask this guy," he nodded at the other old cowboy. "Ramón he was a...how you call it in English? ... un vaquero qué rodea el ganado."

"A wrangler, hombre," said Ramón, "a wrangler." Then he nodded at Jefe, saying, "This guy he's gettin' too old. He don't remember nothin' no more." He chuckled and pulled out a cigarette paper.

"But he tells the truth, this old guy," Ramón nodded. "There was vaqueros all around here in the old days," he was spilling tobacco from a little white sack onto the paper. "When we was young, this place was cattle country. They used to send cows here from all over to fatten them up. This place it was full of cowboys."

"Real cowboys?" I asked.

"The best," replied Jefe. "Just like your abuelo."

Mr. Samuelian nodded. "I have read about them in local history books. Yes, this was quite a place, and these two were famous vaqueros, Manuel."

"They were famous?" Even though I like them, it was hard to believe they could have been famous or anything. I mean, they were just two old guys from the neighborhood. I really enjoyed the stories about my grandpa, but all I could remember of him was sitting on his lap on that couch in front of the house with some other old guys, them smoking those hand-rolled cigarettes and talking. I was too little to understand what they talked about. Then one day my abuelo was gone, and we were at this green cemetery with a whole bunch of people, and flowers all around, and my Mama was crying, so I cried too.

"These two are mentioned in books I read, especially those by a man named Aronold R. Rojas. He's the chronicler of the vaqueros, and he wrote wonderful books."

"No lie?" I didn't know anybody whose name was in books, or at least I didn't think I did. It seemed sort of far-fetched. Jefe said to Ramon, "You remember that guy Rojas? Didn't he work at the Circle 6?"

"No, hombre, he was at Rancho San Emedio when we knew him, then he opened that stable out by Oildale, the Bar-O he called it because he had to borrow the money to buy it." The men chuckled. "He was a good hand," Ramon added, "but I didn't know he could write."

"Didn't he pal with that big colored vaquero that spoke real good Spanish, the one that worked at San Emidio? What was that guy's name?" asked Jefe.

"This guy he don't remember nothin'," Ramon grinned. "Richard, was his name, hombre, Richard Shaw."

Jefe ignored the barb. "Well, one time I was downtown in Bakersfield, and I seen Richard Shaw, and he was all bandaged up. I asked if he was in a wreck or something, and he told me that somebody'd bet him the dollars he couldn't rope and hog-tie a badger out there. 'Well,' he told me, 'I roped one and tied it and I won the ten dollars, but I had to pay the doctor twenty to patch me up. And it bit my horse; it cost me five more to have old Rags patched up. Those're some mean critters, and expensive too.'" That got the men to laughing once more.

Just then from down the street we heard this loud snarling and growling, then some high yips. "What's that?"

asked Mr. Samuelian. A few seconds later, Flaco's champion Rollo dashed by still yipping and looking like an old-time movie being shown way too fast. Nothing followed him, but Rollo didn't know that. He just kept running, not even looking back.

We all glanced at one another. 'Maybe that dog he found a badger," suggested Ramon.

"Aren't you two supposed to round up cattle in the foothills soon?" my neighbor asked the two vaqueros. "Maybe you should take that dog with you to protect you from coyotes. He's pretty quick."

"Yeah," grinned Jefe, "but he's quick in the wrong direction. I kinda like ugly dogs, though, and that sure is one."

We all laughed, then Ramon said, "Me and this old man we're gonna help old Dick Scaramella round up his stock up at Pozo Flat like we do every year. There's not much more real cowboyin' to do around here — all farms, all houses, and those big malls. Too many people," he shook his head, sadly I thought.

"It was good when we was young, though," added Jefe. "We was lucky."

"Yes," agreed Mr. Samuelian, "perhaps we all were," and those three men smiled at one another is a way I couldn't quite understand.

## Chapter 24
# The Promise

I was coming home from school later because we'd started having seventh-grade basketball practice on one of the outdoor courts after classes every day. The eighth-grade boys' team, the seventh-grade girls and eighth-grade girls used the other three.

Tran turned out to be the best seventh-grade player in the whole Catholic-school league that year. Because of him, Our Lady of Guadalupe's Saints actually made the finals of the playoff against the St. Francis Colts, the only team in our league we lost to during the regular season. Guadalupe didn't manage that kind of basketball success very often.

If Linda's practice ended before mine, she'd wait for me, and if mine ended first, I'd wait for her, even if Flaco and Keeny made faces and said stupid stuff. Linda and me we walked home together almost every day, holding hands, my heart pounding each time. But I felt bad sometimes too, because I didn't want to have dirty thoughts about her, but I sure had them. I really wanted to think about her like the lovers in movies or songs, all nice and stuff, but no matter how I tried — even when I said lots of Hail Marys to myself — my pants would get all tight when I was close

119

to her. I just couldn't help it.

But I wasn't going to avoid Linda over that, sin or no sin. I went to Confession on Saturdays and kept walking her home after school. The more I knew Linda, the more I wanted to be with her. I'd even find excuses not to say goodbye right away, but finally I always had to.

After walking her home, most days I'd meet Alphabet and Avila at Mr. Samuelian's yard to study. Flaco and Keeny were on the team with me, but they didn't come by so often after my neighbor'd chewed them out for teasing Robert.

Crazy as it sounds, Alphabet and Avila were getting to be buddies, and Tran was showing the ex-bully some kick-fighting moves. He was showing me, too, for that matter. I wasn't trying to be a tough guy or anything, but I'd learned from what happened at the movie theater that I had to be able to defend myself. Even Mr. Samuelian, who was opposed to all kinds of violence, agreed that it was necessary to be able to fight back if you were attacked. "It is a sad truth," he told me, "that there are still bullies in the world like the evil Nizibian. It is also true that when Nizibian encountered the wrath of a just man, he retired from his bullying."

As he often did, he paused and seemed to think, then said, "But I know another bully who responded to reason and respect, don't you?"

It took me a second, but I got it. "Yeah, David Avila before."

"David Avila before," he agreed. "We need to understand why people act the way they do, and try to help them. I'll bet those boys who attacked you at the theater" — I had told him about that experience —" were themselves victims...of racism, of brutality, of something that made them act cruelly."

"It sure did," I agreed, "because they were mean as

tomcats." That made me think of something else. "Were Jefe and Ramón really tough guys?"

"Tough guys?" he smiled. "Oh, I don't think so, not in the cowboy-movie sense anyway — they weren't fighting all the time, shooting six-guns. No, but they were good men who tried to do the right thing. That makes anyone formidable."

"Formidable?" I asked.

"Powerful," he explained.

"Those two old guys..."

My neighbor smiled. "Well, those two are only old guys now, Manuel. Once they were young men. Once they were famous vaqueros. And once this town was the wild west, full of horses and cattle and, yes, men wearing guns like they do in movies."

"Just like in the movies?"

"Yes, except what you see in movies are actors. Jefe and Ramón and your grandfather were the authentic thing, and so was this town, Bakersfield. Let me tell you a bit of history I recently read.

"In 1903, ten years before I was born, there was a gunfight right downtown near where you boys go to the movies. An outlaw gunned down the City Marshall and his deputy. But that wasn't all: the outlaw was then shot by the deputy's brother, who was also a deputy. It was a terrible tragedy...those young lives wasted.

"The murdered deputy had a son, this book said, younger than you are now. When you see those gunfights in the movies, remember that in real life, people lose their fathers and mothers, their sons and daughters, their husbands and wives. They may look spectacular on the screen, but in reality they aren't much fun. But the son of the dead deputy grew up and became a famous singer at the Metropolitan Opera, Lawrence Tibbett. Can you imagine that? The father was a lawman killed in a shootout on a dusty street here, and the son sang in opera houses all over the world. In Paris. In Rome. In London. In Vienna. Just imagine..."

Well, I guess I really couldn't, but it made me think of something else, "This kid in my class, Joey Castro, his big brother got shot."

"Oh, two or three years ago. A drive-by shooting at the pool hall. He was in a gang, wasn't he? I read about it. Sometimes it seems like this society is going backwards."

"One eighth-grader named Rodriguez, he got kicked out of school because he brought a real gun to class. The police even came to our school. His big brother's in a gang."

"Gangs," said Mr. Samuelian, and he shook his head. "I hope you boys will avoid such nonsense."

"We will." I really meant it, too.

By the time Alphabet and Avila showed up, we had changed the subject. Gangs and stuff seemed like that made Mr. Samuelian real sad. He was the only grown-up I knew who even talked much about those things—most people here always said that kind of stuff only happened in L.A. or New York. But us kids knew better than that. There were beginning to be gangs all over Bakersfield, little ones and big ones.

The other guys and me all worked for a while that afternoon cultivating my neighbor's big, green weeds, stroking their fuzzy stalks and thinning the dead and dried ones. Afterwards, David, Tran and me sat at the small table under Mr. Samuelian's apple tree, and began struggling with algebra. "Es fácil," Tran said — he was using more and more Spanish.

"Al contrario," said Avila, "a mí es muy difícil."

"Me, too," I agreed. "I don't think it's so easy."

Our tutor grinned, then said, "Look, X stands for 3 in this equation because Y stands for 7."

"That part's easy," I said, and I poked Avila.

"Simón," he nodded, winking.

Mr. Samuelian, who was working on a tree in the midst of his jungle, called, "¿Hay problemas?"

"No hay," I said, then I exchanged glances with Avila.

"I'm helping Manuel with the Espanish too," David explained with a grin. "He is muy slow."

I poked him and returned to algebra.

That evening I sat at the kitchen table finishing my English homework, a book report, and wondering how much a telephone call to Alaska might cost—if I could discover my father's number — when the phone rang. I hoped it was one of those miracles like in the movies and my dad would be on the line, him or Linda, so I grabbed it right away. "Hi."

"Hello, honey," my mother said.

"¿Quién es?" my grandmother called from the other room.

"Es Mamacita," I answered.

"'¿Es Mamacita?'" said my mother, a laugh in her voice. "Since when did you talk Spanish?"

I laughed too. "This guy David Avila's teaching me. It's fun. Abuelita likes it, too."

"I'll bet she does. How's school?"

"It's okay. I'm doing good in all my classes, but Mr. Mancuso's kind of boring. I'm still first-string on the basketball team. We lost, just barely, to Lincoln, this public school, in a practice game, but we beat Perpetual Help and St. Joseph's in the league."

"That's wonderful. I'm happy you're enjoying yourself. Your father was a good basketball player in high school."

"Oh," I said. "I wish he could come see me play."

Mom didn't reply for a long time, then she cleared her throat and asked, "Are your friends playing?"

"Yeah, Tran's the best. He scores most of our points.

Flaco's on the first-team too, and Keeny's on the team. He's a sub, and he's not real good. None of the sub's are. David Avila can't play because it's his second year in seventh."

"Has daddy written to you?"

I paused. "Not yet."

"Have you written to him?"

"Well...no, I've kind of forgotten to. I've been real busy with school and basketball and stuff." I suddenly felt guilty because I really had kind of forgotten. I didn't mention that I'd been busy with Linda too. "I lost his address," I said, just realizing it. "Could you give it to me?"

"Of course."

Why hadn't I thought to call her before. "Do you have his phone number?"

"No, not his new one."

"Oh," I said. At least now I'd know which city to call for his phone number.

After she gave the address to me, Mama's voice brightened. "I'm going to be home for a visit this weekend."

"Really? That's great!"

"We'll go out to dinner and go to the movies while I'm there, okay?"

"Okay." By then my grandmother had walked into the kitchen and she stood at my shoulder, saying nothing, but waiting for her chance to talk. "Abuelita wants to talk to you now, Mama," I said. "I'll see you this weekend."

"I love you, honey."

"Me too, Mama."

I sat there and began reading my history homework my mother and grandmother spoke over the telephone, not paying much attention to what was being said, then I heard Abuelita say, "Well, I think he hangs around that Armenian too much. I warn him, and warn him, but he doesn't listen to his grandmother. *You* talk to him." She thrust the telephone receiver into my hand.

"Talk to your mother," she ordered.

"Hi, again," I said.

Mama cleared her throat, then said, "Abuelita doesn't want you hanging around that Mr. Samuelian's yard any more."

"How come?"

"Because he's strange."

"*He's* strange?" I lowered my voice, and said, "Mrs. Alcalá says Abuelita's strange. She's the only one in the neighborhood that doesn't like Mr. Samuelian."

"That's no way to talk." My mother's voice hardened. "It'd be better if you did what your grandmother asks. She's taking care of you and she knows best."

"She doesn't even talk to him. How can she know if he's strange?"

"Is he the one who teaches you to talk back to your elders? You're just a little boy. Your grandmother knows best."

"I'm a boy, Mama, but not a little one. I'm thirteen now, taller than you or even Tío Tuti."

She hesitated, then said, "Yes, you're growing up, but please obey Abuelita. It'll make life easier for all of us. Don't make me have to order you like a small child."

I knew I couldn't do what she was asking, so she was forcing me to lie. "I'll try," I said.

"Promise?"

"I promise I'll try

That terrible dream returned. My mother with tears or blood or something streaming from her eyes, and me not able to help her, and trying to find my dad in that snow or sand at the same time. I felt like I was sinking in it, drowning, choking. Then I saw Linda and there was this big flash as my body surged, and I felt real, real good just as I woke up.

At first I thought I'd wet the bed, but when I looked I realized what it was, and I said a real fast Act of Contrition, then made my own bed so Abuelita wouldn't see the sheets. Now even my dreams were dirty.

➢

## Chapter 25
# Championship Game

Everyone was surprised that the seventh-grade boys had finished second place to St. Francis in round-robin play, and then won our games in the post-season tournament too. Guadalupe's other teams were eliminated in the first round of their tourneys. I was a starter along with Tran, Flaco, Gary Benevidez, and Luther Dupree. Keeny only got to play when we were way ahead or way behind.

Anyways, we were scheduled to play the St. Francis Colts at Garces Memorial's gym as a warm-up for that Catholic high school's big game against Bakersfield on Friday night. I was supercharged when I realized that we'd actually be using a real gym just like the pro's did, but dumb Flaco ruined it.

"Hey, they're just gonna beat us again, ese," he said.

"No they aren't!"

"Essssse! They got four bloods on their team and we only got Luther...and Tran."

"That's dumb, Flaco. How many black guys you got doesn't matter. Besides how'd Tran get to be a black guy?'"

"My mom says his father was a nigger soldier."

"Hey, I told you before I don't like that word."

"That's still what she said."

127

"I don't care. Mr. Samuelian says that's a word people use to hurt other people, so don't say it to me, and don't say it about a friend."

He kind of sneered. "Besides, ese, those guys eat dogs."

"What guys?"

"Those Vietnam guys, they eat dogs. My cousin in L.A. he told me that. His gang beat up a bunch of 'em, and they call 'em dog-eaters. They can't fight good like us Mexicans."

I didn't know why he was talking so crazy that day, but I was getting mad. "I'll tell Tran and Phuc what you said, pendejo. Maybe, I'll bring them over to visit Rollo."

He squared his little shoulders and sneered. "I could take Phuc. I bet you five dollars" — he said it like "fi' dollahs" so I knew he was imitating the big, bad cousins he always bragged about. "I could knock that chump out. Rollo could tear his throat out."

"Yeah," I challenged, "right after you take his shoes out of your ears. Knock off the bullshit, Flaco, before I knock *you* out. Besides, even if Tran's father was a black guy, how does that make him black. You guys say I'm not a Mexican, but my mother is."

"That's different, ese."

"That's stupid!" Sometimes I hated to even talk to Flaco. He was bouncing like a boxer, that habit of his, hands all low and floppy. "Stand still," I said. "If I'm only half Irish and you call me Irish, and Tran's half Vietnamese why don't you call him Vietnamese? How come being black or Irish counts more?"

"Hey, man, don't you know nothin'? Tran's *black*, ese, a nig...," he stopped himself from saying the N-word, "a black dude."

"And you're a stupid dude." I snapped. "Not half-stupid, all stupid." I was getting real mad. "Don't talk about my friends that way, Flaco. Without Tran we wouldn't be in the championship game."

"I won't even be at the game, vato," he sneered. "I'm goin' to L.A. with my mother and little sister to visit my tia and cousins. We're leavin' tomorrow, so I won't be here."

"Flaco, it's for the *title*! We're gonna play at the high school. It'll be awesome! You can sleep over at my house if you want, but you can't miss the game. We need everyone if we're gonna win." I did my best to persuade him.

"No way, vato. Exspecially because we're gonna lose anyway." He acted like he wanted me to beg him.

That did it. "No we're not, pendejo!" I shouted, and I pushed his chest so hard that he kind of floated backward. I had grown a lot bigger than him. I was the second tallest on the team behind Luther.

"Hey, watch it, pendejo!" he hollered back, but he didn't advance.

"Get out of here, you little chicken," I spat. "We don't need chickens on the team."

"Oh yeah," he said, walking away, "you're gonna lose!"

"Come back here and say that!"

"Kiss off!" he shouted and he sprinted away.

If he'd turned around I'd have punched him even if he was my friend, that's how mad I was. Great, I thought, just great! One of our players not even showing up for the game. I could imagine what Father Mario, our coach, was going to say.

Just then Keeny came out of the multi-purpose room, and asked, "What's wrong, ese? Your face is purple."

"Pendejo Flaco's gonna miss the game Friday," I said.

He grinned like he was real happy. "I know," he said. "I'll probably get to start."

"Yeah," I said. I knew what that meant. Keeny could hardly dribble the ball, and he couldn't shoot at all. I don't think he'd even scored a point all season. But he was better than our other substitutes: fat Anthony Martinez, Chuy Bernal, Joaquin Sandoval, Phuc Nguyen, and the Dominguez twins, Tommy and Terry. In fact, Abuelita was probably better than any of them. "Let's go practice shooting," I said. He needed it.

What I was thinking, but didn't say because I didn't want to hurt Keeny's feelings, was that Linda was really good enough to be a starter on the seventh grade boys' team. She was better than dumb Flaco, a lot better than Keeny and the rest. She beat me at H-O-R-S-E as often as I beat her, so I knew she could shoot, and she was real quick when we played one-on-one. I even thought about that movie where a girl painted a mustache on her lip and passed for a guy, but that was only a dumb movie. Linda already looked like a real girl with, you know, boobs and everything, so no way they'd let her play.

That Friday some of my neighbors arranged a car-pool to come see the game, and uncle Tuti brought my grandmother. Linda was there, too, and she waved at me during the warm-ups.

Things were great. The high school's pep band was playing, and the ninth-grade cheerleaders from Garces were there too. The gym wasn't even half full when our game started, but by the second half lots of high-school kids and more adults were arriving for the varsity match that would be played when ours finished. To me, it was a huge crowd.

In the first 30 seconds, we brought the ball down and set up our offense. Luther was playing low post, and we got the ball into him, then he fired it out to me, and I bounced a pass to Alphabet. When he feinted and drove for the basket, the whole Colt team surrounded him. At the last second, he fired a pass behind his back to me, and I laid it in without any of their players near me. "Cover that guy!" I heard their coach yell. That was the only field goal I scored in the first half, because the Colts put one of their good players on me.

We managed to keep the game close, playing a zone defense so none of their guys got to work on Keeny man-to-man. It was like playing four against five, but Tran was hot — he must've scored nearly 20 points before half-time. St. Francis used its bigger kids to score inside pretty easy. Me and Luther did our best to block out, but they had three guys taller than him, so they snagged most of the boards and got most of the fast breaks.

As Father Mario instructed, we slowed the game's pace down as much as we could, set screens for Tran, then tried to be available for passes when the Colts double- or triple-teamed him. Anyways, we kept it close and in the fourth quarter we actually tied St. Francis when Tran hit three short jumpers in a row, while they went cold. The best basket of all came when we had the ball out of bounds under their basket. Poor Keeny was confused and he had his back turned, so Tran inbounded and tossed the ball against Keeny's rear, caught the bounce, and scored a lay-in.

"That's not legal!" their coach shouted, but the officials disagreed. The Colts called time out, and when we jogged to the sidelines, Linda caught my eye, smiled and waved. The crowd was cheering like mad, and I saw my Uncle Tuti jumping up and down. I honestly thought we'd win.

Then things fell apart: Alphabet twisted his ankle and Luther fouled out. That meant Terry Dominguez and Phuc Nguyen had to play.

With minute or so left—we were falling behind again—I managed to grab a defensive rebound and whip a pass out to Benevidez, who then tossed it to Keeny on a fast break. The St. Francis fans in the stands started chanting "Four! Three! Two! One!" like the clock was running down, and poor Keeny believed them. He stopped about half-court, thinking the game was over I guess, and the white guy on their team slapped the ball away from him, dribbled it back into our court, and scored on a give-and-go. We lost by 12.

The Colts were good sports. "Nice game," several of them said to me as we slapped hands, and their coach even congratulated me: "Good D, son. You really made us work in the middle."

We still lost, but you wouldn't have known it by the way my uncle was acting. "Hey Manny! Great game! Great game, right Mama? Manny can really play!"

"It was so rough," Abuelita said, "and noisy in this place too."

"No kiddin', Manny", my uncle said, "you really played good, just like me when I was your age."

I was searching the crowd milling on the court for Linda, then she appeared next to me with two other girls from our class. "You guys played so good," she said, touching my sweaty arm, and my gym shorts got tight right away even with my grandmother standing there.

"Thanks," I said. "Wasn't Tran awesome? We almost beat those guys." I turned toward my grandmother and uncle, and said, "This is my friend Linda and her friends Maria and Lourdes." The girls nodded and smiled, as I said to them, "This is my grandma and my Uncle Tuti."

Grandma puckered her face like an old apple as she examined the girls, but Uncle Tuti grinned. "Nice to meet you," he said, shaking hands with them. "How'd you like the game?"

"I just wish we'd won," said Lourdes.

"You played really good, Manuel," Linda said, her eyes on me in a way that made my chest fill up too.

"Thanks." I was still pumped up over the game, so I said right in front of everyone, "Can I sit with you for the high-school game, Linda?"

Everybody at school knew she was my girlfriend, but I'd never said anything in front of grown-ups before. She appeared startled for a second, then her cinnamon skin took on a deeper red glow as she said, "Sure."

"Great! I'll be out soon as I shower."

"You are not going to sit with your own abuela?" Grandma asked, her face drooping like hot ice-cream.

Uncle Tuti winked at me and shook his head. "We're going home, Mama," he said. "One game's enough for us."

"Oh," said my grandmother, and she gazed at me strangely.

"You two kids enjoy the next one. Give me a call when it's over and I'll come pick you up. Oh, Manny, here's that five bucks I owe you. You can buy yourselves some popcorn." He handed me a bill and winked.

He was sure a nice uncle.

"You owed Manuel some money?" asked my grandmother.

Uncle Tuti just grinned and said, "It's a long story, Mama."

In the locker room, Keeny was sitting and looking at the floor. "I lost the game for us, ese," he said.

"No way!" I told him. "If anybody did, it was Flaco. You showed up and did the best you could, ese. Hey, I made more mistakes than you." I had, too, because I'd touched the ball a lot more. Things go real fast in a game, and Keeny hadn't played much at all during the season. It had been hard for him to figure out what was happening, but he'd stayed where he was supposed to in our zone defense and had done his best to keep out of the way on offense.

"Play good, Keeny," Alphabet slapped his back. "Really."

Father Mario had us say a prayer of thanks that nobody on either team seriously injured, then he said, "Even though we lost the game, you boys didn't quit.

"I am going to award two player-of-the-game certificates tonight, but I wish I could give one to each of you. Tran Nguyen will receive one for his outstanding performance, and Joaquin Padilla will receive one for his inspirational play."

The rest of us cheered: "Way to go, Alphabet! Way to go, Keeny!"

The coach wasn't finished. "I am also going to do something unusual next week. I am going to give each of you boys a basketball of your own — call them game balls — because I'm so proud of all of you. And each of you, whether you got in the game or not, will be awarded a block-G for your efforts tonight and this season."

He didn't say anything about Flaco. I hoped that pendejo would get a block-P.

➤

## Chapter 26
# Flaco Returns

None of us said much to the pendejo when he re-turned from L.A., wearing a bandana on his head like a pirate and trying to act bad.

"I knew we'd lose, anyway, man," he sneered.

I just shook my head. He was getting to be such a boca grande.

"Maybe if we'd've had more niggers..."

"Shut up!" I snapped, and I grabbed his shirt and pulled him close. "What'd I tell you about that word? Don't say that around me any more, Flaco. *Get it*?"

His eyes got real big, and he gulped, "Chill out, Manuel. Chill out, man."

I released him. "I'll chill you out, quitter. See if you get a block G for basketball."

That shocked him. I guess he hadn't heard about what the coach had said after the game. "What do you mean, man? I was first-string!"

"You were no-string for the big game, pendejo. You quit the team when you didn't show up for the champion-ship."

"No way!"

"Ask Keeny."

Flaco kind of sneered, "That's not fair. Besides, Keeny's just a bench-warmer."

"Oh yeah," I snapped, "it wasn't fair for you to skip the game, ese. At least he showed up and played his best. He's not chicken like you."

He backed up, then said, "Yeah, well my cousin showed me a real gun in L.A., man! A real gun! They don't fiddle around with any dumb basketball! They get respec', man!"

"Yeah," I replied, "well you don't get any from me, chicken. You let us down."

"You couldn't say that to my cousin, man! He's a bad dude!"

"If he needs a gun, I could. And I'm saying it to you, pendejo."

I jerked Flaco's bandana off and dropped it on the ground.

"You better watch it, vato!" he threatened when he thought I couldn't hear him, but I just kept walking away.

Right after that Avila spied him and called him gutless. Then Tran chewed on him. Then Luther. Then Phuc and Benevidez called him down. By the time that Monday was over, Flaco wasn't wearing his tough-guy bandana, but I noticed that Keeny was sort of following him around again.

The coach did what he said he'd do. On Friday we had an assembly at noon in the Multi-Purpose Room, and he gave block letters and regulation basketballs to all the players who'd suited up for the championship game. The school got a plaque for us finishing second in the league, and Alphabet was given the team's Most Valuable Player Award and an All-League certificate. I got the Most Improved, and Luther was the Most Inspirational. Flaco got zip. It was awesome.

Best of all, Linda was the Most Valuable Player on the girls' team. We walked home together that day, and she carried her trophy and my plaque. "I was real proud of you, Manuel," she said.

"Hey, I was proud of you. You were better than any-one on your team or our team, except for Tran, I mean."

She giggled. "No I wasn't. You played harder teams than we did. Everybody on that St. Francis boys team was better than any player in our whole league. They were so big and so fast, but you played real good against them, Manuel. I'm glad Father Mario gave you this award."

"Yeah, I am too. Our team really did improve. Last week, we even beat the eighth-graders when we scrim-maged them."

"But why'd Flaco quit the team?"

The mention of his name upset me, but I said only, "I don't know, he's been acting weird lately. He wants to be a bad-ass or something."

"Maybe it's because he's kind of little."

He hadn't grown much since sixth grade, but that didn't excuse him. Lots of the boys in our class besides Flaco were smaller than some of the girls—Benevidez, Phuc, Zepeda, Bernal, both the Dominguezes, and some oth-ers—but they didn't act like pendejos.

In fact, our whole class was pretty weird: a couple of guys like Avila already had muscles and the beginnings of mustaches, and a couple of the girls like Carmen had big breasts and were as tall as grown women, but others looked like second graders — little skinny sticks. Linda and me weren't sticks, but we weren't all grown-up-looking like Avila and Carmen, either, so I guess we were lucky. We were both big for the class, but not giants.

That evening a junior-high dance was scheduled for the multi-purpose room, and I planned to meet Linda there. My grandmother wasn't sure I should go. "A dance, for little children like you?" she asked. She was standing next to me, looking up at my face.

"Hey, grandma, I'm in junior high now. I'm a teenager."

"I don't know, mi'jito, I just don't know. When I was a girl..."

I had carefully combed my hair, and I was wearing a new shirt Mom had sent me. I planned to walk to the dance with Keeny, Avila and Tran. "You can come to the dance, too, if you want. They need chaperones."

She slowly sat at the small kitchen table. "I think you'd better stay home with your grandmother. Your uncle Arturo used to go to those dances, and look how he behaves, like los otros...never comes to visit his mother."

I couldn't believe it. "Grandma...," I pleaded. It had never occurred to me that she'd do something like this.

"No, you can stay home with me. We can light a candle and pray for your purity." Her jaw was jutting, so I knew that she'd made up her mind. I also knew that Keeny would be by any minute.

"Grandma, it's a school dance. The nuns will be there. Father Mario will be there."

Something like a sneer crossed her face. "Nuns do not attend dances. Priests do not attend dances. Do not lie to your grandmother. And I suppose you'll want to dance with *girls* at that dance, too," she said.

"I'm not gonna dance with guys."

"Don't be disrespectful. You need to pray to the Holy Mother for your purity."

"I'm not impure." I wondered what all this purity stuff was about all of a sudden. Had she found the stains on my sheets?

"Always thinking about girls. Sitting with that Cuban girl at the basketball game..."

"I'm not always thinking about girls. And Linda's my friend, and besides she's not a Cuban. She's an American like me." What the heck was wrong with Grandma? To me, she was acting muy lunatica. Not knowing what else I could do, I picked up the phone and dialed my mother's number. I knew she'd tell Abuelita to let me go to the dance.

"And who are you calling now?" Abuelita asked. "Some girl?"

"Mama."

"Ahhh," she seemed to brush me off with one hand. "She went to those dances, and look who she married."

Mama didn't answer — she wasn't home, I guess. All of a sudden I felt like crying, but my grandma just sat there with her jaw stuck out.

I walked into the bathroom and locked the door and stood in front of the mirror looking at myself— my freckles, my light hair, my pale skin, the pimples on my nose and chin — kind of ugly, I guess.

I couldn't miss this chance to dance with Linda; it might be the last time a cute girl would ever want to be with an ugly guy like me, but now I wasn't even going to the dance. I'd never find another girl as cool and pretty and fun as Linda, and she would be waiting for me, but I wasn't going to get to go. The best day of my life was turning into the worst one.

Then another idea occurred to me. Why hadn't I thought of Uncle Tuti? I returned to the telephone — Abuelita still sat there, but now she had her Rosary beads out, and she said, "Get your Rosary, Manuel, and come pray with your grandmother. You don't need those dances."

Thank heaven Uncle Tuti was home. When I explained what was happening, he said, "Okay, I'll come over. There's no point in me trying to talk to Mama over the phone. When she acts like that, I need to deal with her face-to-face. Don't worry, you'll get to go to the dance. And Manny, you really did play a good game the other night. I'm sorry your folks didn't see it."

I sighed, "Me, too."

To soothe her, I knelt with Abuelita and prayed while I waited for my uncle, but I couldn't concentrate.

"Hey Maaan-ny!" echoed through the house. Keeny was standing in the yard and, as usual, he was howling. I was relieved to hear him.

"Who is that?" hissed my grandmother.

"I think it's Keeny."

"Joaquin Padilla. Well, you can send that malcriado away. We are praying."

I rose from my knees and trudged out to the yard. "Hey, vato, you ready?" he called.

"I gotta wait till my uncle gets here."

"How come?"

"Oh, my grandma's acting wigged out."

"Boy," said Keeny, "grown-ups sure can act goofy, can't they ese? My papa came home the other night and said I had to get a haircut. My hair was just the same as always, but he got mad and hollered that I had to cut it off."

I examined him closely. "Your hair looks the same to me," I reported.

"It oughta. My mom hit him with the broom and made him go to bed. She said he'd drunk too much beer with his compañeros."

"With a broom?"

"Yeah. It was great! She chased him too."

It didn't sound all that great to me.

# Chapter 27
# The Dance

As Keeny and me were leaving for the dance, the last thing Uncle Tuti said was, "Don't do anything I wouldn't do," then he winked.

In the background, I heard my grandmother's voice, "Arturo! Arturo! ¡Ven aqui!"

"Yeah, Mama," he called, then he said to me, "You'd better get out of here while you can."

I sure agreed. She was acting so weird that I didn't know what to expect. At least she hadn't resisted after Tío Tuti'd arrived and told her that he'd stay while I went out. "She just doesn't want to be left alone at night," he explained. "Ever since my father died, she's hated nights."

Avila and Alphabet were waiting for Keeny and me in front of the multi-purpose room, and music was drifting out the open doors. They said they were waiting for us, anyway, but I think the real reason they were still outside is because they were scared to go inside until all of us guys were there. Me, too, for that matter, and I had Linda waiting for me, but I was still kind of nervous. This was the first dance ever for me — I'd skipped the one last semester — and somehow it felt different seeing everybody all dressed up in the evening, and with some of their parents all dressed up, too, and seated in folding chairs around the floor, or even dancing.

"You guys missed it," grinned Avila. "They kicked your boy Flaco out."

"Really?" asked Keeny. "What'd he do?"

"He showed up dressed all funny with this big baggy black jacket on and his hair in some kinda net like my mother wears and he had on this giant earring!"

Just then Benevidez came out of the multi-purpose room with a big grin on his face. "Did you hear, ese? Father Mario gave Flaco the boot and said he has to report to the office on Monday. What a pendejo!"

"To the office?" I said. "No lie?"

"No lie."

"Flaco look dumb," Tran added, "like a clown."

"Hey, ese," Benevidez said to me, "there's someone waiting for you inside." All the guys laughed, but not in a mean way.

"Let's go in," I said.

A high-school band — three guitars, a drum, and a piano played by kids, plus a saxophone played by the football coach — was entertaining on the stage at one end of the floor. To me they sounded pretty good. Almost all the seventh-grade boys were on one side of the room and almost all the seventh-grade girls were on the other. The eighth graders were mingling.

Linda sat with Maria and Lourdes, so I hesitated to approach her, although Tran urged, "Go on, ese."

"I will," I said, but this setting made me shy.

I didn't have to as it turned out, because as soon as she saw me, Linda walked over and smiled. She took my hand and led me onto the floor with other dancers, and I began the uncomfortable process of trying to lead while saying under my breath "step, step-together, step."

"I was afraid you weren't coming to the dance," she

said as I continued mumbling the steps under my breath. I held her almost an arm's length away from me and concentrated on my feet. I should've concentrated on hers, since I stepped on them a whole bunch of times, but she didn't get mad.

"We had some trouble at home, but it's okay now," I explained. "Oops! Sorry."

She laughed, then said, "Flaco got kicked out of the dance."

"That's what I heard."

"Patty said he called Father Mario a name."

"Boy, I hope he didn't."

"Me too."

When the tune ended, we stood for a moment on the floor. I didn't want to go back with the guys, and I think she didn't want to go back with the girls, but that's what everyone else was doing. Heck with it, I thought, and I took Linda's hand and led her to where some of the eighth-grade boys and girls were sitting together. Luther Dupree was already over there with Patty Melendez, so we wouldn't be the only seventh-graders.

We joined those two and talked about the basketball game, and how Luther's cousin had been playing for the Colts, and how Patty'd gone to St. Francis School for the first and second grades. A real fast, loud song was being played, so we almost had to shout.

"What's wrong with Flaco?" Dupree finally asked me. "He's been actin' like a fool ever since he missed that game."

"I don't know. I sure wish he hadn't missed it though."

"We all do," nodded Luther. "I told my cousin they were lucky, and he said maybe they were."

"No lie? He said that?"

Another slow tune began and, for some reason, the lights dimmed somewhat. Linda and me walked onto the

143

floor again, and it was a little easier to "step, step-together, step," although I still tramped on her feet a few times. She giggled when I did, so I didn't feel real bad.

The next slow one we tried again and did a little better and danced a little closer, close enough so that I could feel the warmth of her body, although we weren't exactly touching or anything. Father Mario was patrolling the dance floor, and if a couple was too close, he made them move apart. All I know is that Linda and me were close enough so that it made me feel different, real light and kind of breathless at the same time, and I tingled. She smelled so good. I got one of *those* in my pants, so I was glad we weren't dancing any closer. I didn't want Linda to think I was having dirty thoughts.

At ten o'clock they played the last dance. Everyone was on the floor it seemed like, and my girl and me we were kind of lost in the middle, and our bodies were touching — hers was so soft and warm — and in me something like syrup was swelling until I couldn't swallow. My cheek was on her cheek, my arm was around her waist, my nose touched her hair, and I'd forgotten all about "step, step-together, step." I only cared about how we moved, and my pants were real tight.

Then I heard Father Mario. "That's a little too close."

It was like waking up. "Huh?" I said. Both our bodies went stiff.

He didn't sound mean or mad or anything, but he said, "Not quite so close, kids."

"Yes, Father," we said, and separated. But not really, because even dancing a little ways apart, I felt closer to her than ever before. We held hands after the music stopped.

➤

## Chapter 28
# Vaqueros

$F$laco had spent most of the week in after-school detention, but he was a minor celebrity at school — the kid who'd talked back to Father Mario. He always claimed his cousins down in L.A. were big-time gang-bangers, and now he was really swaggering around school. I still didn't even believe all the stuff he said about his cousins, because he always liked to tell stories to make himself sound bad.

I was kind of surprised to find him standing in front of my house when I went outside the next Saturday morning. "Hey, man," he said, "wanta go shoot some baskets?" He was wearing a new Raiders T-shirt and some baggy pants, and he'd slicked his hair back and pulled a black net over it.

"Sure." I guess we were friends again, but I wasn't real comfortable with how he looked. Dressing like that was like a challenge to other guys, maybe to big guys.

"Check out my ear," he said.

I did and saw it was pierced, and that he wore a small silver stud.

"That's cool," I told him, but what's that goo in your hair?"

"That's not goo, man, that's setting gel. It cost me six

bucks. And I got this boss shirt at K-Mart...a blue-light special, man."

"You look different."

"You know my cousin Chacho, he said maybe I could get colors with his gang, man and look what else I got." He held up a spray can. "I'm gonna tag some walls for the gang, man."

"Well don't get caught *man*. How come you're saying 'man' all the time?"

"Don't you know how gang guys talk, man? My cousin Julio, he's even got a bunch of tattoos."

"Where's Keeny?" I asked.

"He had to go to the store with his mother, man. He's gonna come over after."

We dribbled the ball I'd got from Father Mario and passed it back and forth as we walked toward Guadalupe. "Hey, you know those two old guys, Jefe and Ramón, that come over to Mr. Samuelian's?" I said.

"Yeah."

"They used to be real cowboys."

"Those old guys? No way, man. They're too old."

"Hey, Flaco," I said, "people aren't always old. They have to be young first."

"They don't have to be cowboys first, man."

"Mr. Samuelian said they were. And he said there were lots of cowboys called vaqueros around here in the olden days. Even my grandpa..."

Flaco halted and held the ball. "Right, man," he said. "Your grandpa was a bad cowboy, sure, and there used to be lots of Indians in Bakersfield too, I suppose. *Right.*"

"You don't have to be a smart ass!" I snapped. I didn't mind him disagreeing with me, but his tone made me mad. He kind of blinked when I challenged him, so I relaxed and said, "Besides, your tía told me your grandpa was an Indian."

Flaco kind of snorted, "Yeah, but not a real one, man, with feathers and stuff like in the movies. He just sat around and smoked and talked to other old guys. He was real old, too."

"Pendejo, you have to be old to be grandpa. He wasn't always old, either."

None of the other guys showed up at the court, so we played H-O-R-S-E and 21 until we got tired, then some guys from La Loma showed up and started ragging Flaco about his outfit. They were wearing what looked like real gang colors, so Flaco and me went home.

On the way back we ran into Keeny. "Where're you guys goin', man? I thought we were gonna shoot baskets?" He was dressed different too. He had on this Pendleton shirt buttoned at his throat and a net over his hair. He'd put goo on his hair, too, so it shined like black plastic.

"Oh, some of those pendejos from La Loma came over, man," Flaco said, swaggering his shoulders. "I called 'em down, man, but they didn't want no parts of me, so we came home."

Big liar. He'd wet his pants when those La Loma guys'd ragged him, but now he was acting like he was bad. "Hey, Flaco," I said, "we can go back if you want."

Keeny puffed up a little bit, swaggered his own shoulders and sorta threw his hands down like the black rappers do on MTV. "Oh, yeah. Maybe I could beat 'em up, too, man." Sometimes it seemed like Flaco and Keeny were twins: the fabulous pendejo brothers.

I laughed at both of them. "Those guys were bigger than Avila," I said. "Don't talk dumb."

"Hey," Flaco ignored me and said to Keeny, his voice changing back to normal, "Ryan claims those two old guys, Ramón and Jefe, they used to be real cowboys, man."

"Mr. Samuelian said they were," I added.

Ramón and Jefe, they used to be real cowboys, man."

"Mr. Samuelian said they were," I added.

Keeny said, "They're too old, man. Besides how does he know."

Here we go again, I thought. "He read about them in a book."

"Those two old pendejos are in a book? The phone book maybe," added Keeny.

"Okay," I said, "let's go ask Mr. Samuelian."

"Okay, man," agreed Flaco.

"Okay man!" said Keeny.

As we marched toward my neighbor's house, those two were swinging their shoulders, each trying to out-bad-ass the other. It occurred to me that most of what I did with them anymore was argue. Fortunately, Mr. Samuelian was home.

"Where are you two going," he immediately asked Flaco and Keeny, "to some kind of costume party? My wife used to wear a little ear stud like that," he added.

Mr. Samuelian had a funny look on his face, but he didn't say any more about their appearances. "Have you boys ever noticed how clothes define people?" he asked. "For example, Tran's mother still wears traditional Vietnamese clothing at the family's store because in her heart she will always be Vietnamese. And I, I dress like an eccentric old man," he chuckled.

"What's eccentric?" I asked.

"Oh, it's just a fancy word for odd," he continued chuckling.

"Anyways," I said, "we came over because I wanted you to show these guys that book with Jefe and Ramón in it. They don't believe me."

Mr. Samuelian disappeared into his house, then returned with a book titled Our Hispanic Heritage and he showed us a chapter "Vaqueros." Then he said, "Let me

148

tional among them. Skill was a minimum requirement of their jobs.

" 'Manuel Higuera' — that's Manuel's grandfather — 'could put a dollar on each stirrup and ride a bucking horse without losing either coin. I have many times seen the wrangler Ramón Contreras' — that's our Ramón, boys — 'pick his battered body off the ground when bucked off by a wild horse and climb on again for a repeat performance; he never quit. Juan Perez, nearly ninety, could rope a hundred calves before he missed a throw. Tiny, shriveled old Avelino Martinez tucked a six-shooter into his belt and took no guff from anyone of any size or age. Jefe Lopez' — that's our Jefe — 'the legendary trail boss, no matter how fatigued, always sat quietly on his horse until all his men had been fed before dismounting to feed himself.'

"There's more, but that's the important part. That's your heritage, boys. Manuel's grandfather and our friends, the vaqueros Ramón Contreras and Jefe Lopez were great men, my boys, special men."

Flaco made a face. "Those old guys? Did they shoot guns like in the movies?" I guess he thought his gun-toting cousins were the only great men.

"They didn't need to," replied my neighbor. He showed the book to Flaco, then to Keeny, saying, "This very weekend they're rounding up cattle at the Scaramella ranch near Glenville." He added, "you boys should also be proud because your Mexican ancestors were the best cowboys in the world. White cowboys learned from them."

"How come that's not in the movies?" demanded Flaco.

Mr. Samuelian sighed. "That's a very long story. Let's just say that white people make the movies. But in reality, Mexicans were the best, and probably still are. Be proud of Avelino Martinez and Juan Perez and Victor Ortega and all the rest.

Flaco winked at Keeny, then asked, "Were there any

Irish vaqueros, like Ryan?"

My neighbor grinned at me. "As a matter of fact, according to this book there were many Irish ... or part Irish." He fingered through pages for a moment, then said, "Listen to this: 'In those days, English was a strange and foreign tongue in the hills and valleys of California, but many riders whose families had come from Ireland to the Untied States or Mexico made their way to these ranges. Well known were Johnny Congdon, Mickey Wicklow, Jack Flood, and Vester Conlin. Still others were mixtures such as Juan Terrell from Sonora or Sean Garcia from Sinaloa. The famous Obregon family from Sonora was originally named O'Brien....' Well, it goes on from there. So Manuel could very well have vaqueros on both sides of his family."

"Hah!" I said.

"You don't have to be John Wayne or Clint Eastwood to be a real cowboy," said Mr. Samuelian.

"You sure do in the movies, though," Keeny commented.

Just then we heard a tough gang-banger's little sister calling: "Flaaaaaco! Flaaaaaco! My mother wants you!"

Flaco swaggered off, saying, "See you, man."

Then I heard my own mother's voice: "Manuel!" I'd forgotten that she would be arriving for a visit.

"That's my mom," I said, rapidly. "Here, Mom! See you guys."

## Chapter 29
# The Visit

"I thought I asked you not to go to that Mr. Samuelian's yard any more," Mom demanded even before hugging me.

"He was telling us about vaqueros. Did you know Grandpa and Jefe and Ramón were cowboys?"

"Of course I knew Papa was a vaquero. Don't change the subject. And who're Jefe and Ramón?"

"They're two friends of Mr. Samuelian's. Old cowboys that knew Grandpa."

"Ohhh...those two. Sure I remember them. They were nice to me when I was little." She gazed at me then and shook her head. "Give me a kiss, mijo. I didn't come home to punish you, but you must obey grandma. That Samuelian is dangerous Don't you understand it causes trouble with my mother?"

"He's not, Mama," I said. "Honest."

"Is that Manuel?" I heard Abuelita ask from the porch. "Some *girl* wants him the phone."

"Linda?"

"Yes, I think so."

"A girl?" my mother asked. "Calling you?"

"I've gotta go answer," I said.

While Linda and me were talking, I heard my mother and grandmother in the other room. "He's growing up so fast," Mom said, "and I'm not here with him. He looks a foot taller. I've decided to come back home soon, Mama. I'm sure I can find some work here. I should be with my son." I surged when I heard her say that and I told Linda. She said it was neat.

When we hung up, I hurried into the living room and my mother grinned at me. "What's this? A girlfriend, Manuel?"

"Kind of," I said.

"He's too young to talk to girls, mija," said my grandmother. "Tell him not to. Besides, that girl is one of those Cubans."

"So what?" I said.

Mama walked across the room and put her arms around me. "Oh, I think it's all right to talk with girls, Mama, even Cubans." She smiled, then said, "Remember the crush I had on Jaime Herrera in the seventh grade?"

Abuelita said, "When I was a girl..."

"I know, things were different," grinned my mother.

"They certainly were." Abuelita did not smile. "And your son hangs around the yard of that crazy Armenian, too."

"I've talked to him about that, and he promised not to."

"No, I didn't," I said.

"What do you mean, you didn't? I heard you."

"No, Mama, I only promised that I'd try not to."

"Well, now I want you to promise not to. I've had enough of this." She suddenly sounded mad.

"And he runs around with bad boys, too," added my grandmother.

"No, I don't!"

"Manuel! Don't talk back to your Grandmother that way!" warned my mom.

"It is all the work of the madman," hissed Abuelita.

I started to argue, but held my tongue. I didn't want to make my mother angry and have her leave me again. I turned toward Mom and said, "Mr. Samuelian's the only man I've got to talk to now that Daddy's gone."

Her face suddenly softened, like she might cry, and I wished I hadn't said that.

Abuelita snapped, "He can call Arturo if he wants to talk to a man. He can talk to the priest."

"Tuti's got his own life, Mama. Manuel does need a man to talk to," said my mother. "He's growing up."

For some reason Abuelita seemed real angry that day. "And at that school they are teaching Godless evolution!"

Mama ignored her.

"School doesn't teach you everything," Abuelita snorted, still sounding like she wanted an argument.

"Well, if I had a better education, I'd be able to find a better job," said my mother. "I know that much."

Sometimes I thought Grandma wanted me to earn good grades but not to learn anything. "And he reads books! Do you know that your son now says that one of those ah...ah...como se llamas...little boxes for cooking..."

"Microwaves," I said.

"Yes. He claims those things can heat without fire! With invisible flames, I suppose. Like Satan himself!"

My mother smiled. "I have a small one in Los Angeles, Mama," she said. "It works."

"Not without flames. No. There is a trick, mija. Do not be fooled. The devil is at work."

"Mr. Samuelian showed us guys in a physics book about how they work," I said.

"Oh, yes, *books!*" said Abuelita. "What did I tell you about the madman!" Then she turned toward me. "A good person doesn't need all those books. Only the Holy Bible is necessary." She rubbed the shiny red cover of the large one she kept near her chair.

153

Well, our conversation sort of ended there. I could tell by looking at my mother that she was wondering if maybe Mrs. Alcala had been right when she'd said Abuelita was getting strange. Mom excused herself to clean up so we could all go out for Chinese food. Soon as she was gone, I snuck over to our neighbor's house.

Mr. Samuelian was sitting in one of his old wooden lawn chairs reading. "Can I ask you a question?" I said.

He looked up and, as usual, smiled. "Of course."

"My grandma says nobody needs to read any book but the Bible. How come we read so many different ones at Catholic school then?"

"The Bible is a wonderful book. I have read it several times and many other sacred texts, too. They are absolutely essential, but they do not contain all wisdom because new wisdom is accumulated each day. They are wonderful starters, Manuel, but not engines.

"God gave us minds to use. We must keep them sharp with new ideas. For instance, even now I am studying new theories of the origin of the cosmos. The mind is a muscle, Manuel, it must be exercised to grow. A closed mind shrivels and disappears."

I thought about that, then something else occurred to me. "Have you ever heard of a guy named Eddie Puss and a lady named la Llorona?"

"Eddie?" he said, then a small smile played across his lips. Finally, he said, "Yes, yes I have."

"Who are they, exactly?"

"Sit down, Manuel, and I'll explain."

The stories he told me about Eddie Puss and la Llorona were as weird as my dreams.

## CHAPTER 30
# "The Mall"

Just when I got totally disgusted with Flaco and decided not to run around with him anymore, he telephoned me. Rollo had got out of the yard again, and this time a car had run over him. He was dead. Poor Flaco almost cried when he told me that. Well, I always kind of liked Rollo when Flaco wasn't bragging about him. That dog strutted around our neighborhood, lifting his leg everywhere. To me he was funny, kind of bouncing when he walked, then streaking low to the ground when a tough hombre like Tuxedo was after him.

Keeny and me we went to Flaco's house and helped dig the hole where he buried Rollo. The dead dog looked little as a doll, but he had dried blood from his ears and mouth, and his eyes were foggy like bad marbles. I got sad and felt like I might cry. When we started piling the dirt on his dog, Flaco couldn't help himself, and tears streamed down his face. I looked away.

After we finished, we got some sticks and made two crosses and wrote "Rollo" on them. We put one on his grave and looped his collar around it, then took the other one to the place where he got run over. We stuck it in the ground on the side of the road. We'd borrowed some pretty flowers from Mrs. Lawrence's yard on the way over, and we put them around it. "Let's go get a candle at the church," Flaco said, "we could put it here for Rollo."

Keeny shook his head, "That might be a sin, ese."

"I don't think God would mind," I disagreed. "I think God likes dogs or He wouldn't make them so much fun."

"You guys go get one," said Keeny. "I gotta go home."

We did that, with Flaco talking about what a chicken pendejo Keeny was all the way.

The night after my mom went back to L.A., Flaco telephoned me, and he was all excited sounding, saying let's us guys go to the mall tomorrow because we don't have school. He didn't say "man" and he didn't talk about guns or being tough or that stuff, so I said okay.

We had a holiday because Catholic-school teachers were holding a big conference, and I really didn't have any plans for what to do that day. Abuelita was acting so grouchy that I sure as heck didn't want to hang around the house. Anyways, Keeny, Flaco, Avila, Tran and me decided we'd all go to this big mall called The Plaza and hang out.

Alphabet was waiting at the bus stop that morning when I got there. He was wearing our Guadalupe School uniform, blue cords and a white shirt. I had on new jeans and a new shirt my mother brought me from L.A. Pretty soon Avila showed up — old jeans and a regular shirt. Then the three of us saw two big-time gang warriors sort of slouching toward us, swinging their shoulders, dragging their arms like gorillas. Flaco was wearing his black t-shirt, baggy britches, and gooey hair; Keeny had on his Pendleton and his hair net. Right behind them was Flaco's little sister. She was wearing a dress.

"How come those pendejos're walking so funny?" asked Avila. "Do they got sore feet?"

"Look funny," agreed Tran.

"Hey, Flaco," I said as soon as he was near enough to hear, "what's with Dolores?"

156

"It's okay, man," he said, "I just gotta take care of her because..."

The little girl interrupted him: "My mother says he has to."

"Her mother says he has to," I said to David and Tran.

"Ha-ha, man," said Flaco as sarcastically as he could.

"Where'd you get that hair-net, Padilla," Avila asked Keeny, "from your mama?"

Keeny made a face, but he didn't answer the formidable Avila.

"Know what? They were practicing," Dolores announced.

"Practicing what?" I asked.

"Shut up, Dolores!" ordered Flaco.

"Walking," she said. "They looked funny."

Alphabet grinned. "Still look funny," he said.

Neither of the gang-warriors responded to him, but Flaco repeated, "Shut up, Dolores!"

"Know what?" the little girl said. "They wrote on their hands too."

Flaco and Keeny did their best to hide their hands, but I saw that they'd inscribed fake gang tattoos with colored pens. "That looks dumb," I said.

"Does not," snapped Flaco.

"Does too."

"Does not, pendejo."

"Uhhhmmm. I'm telling my mother what you said," Dolores.

"Shut up, Dolores!" snapped her brother.

"You shut up, Skinny," hissed Avila. "You guys don't gotta show off. Besides, I want to ask you something. Last night somebody sprayed some paint n the boxcar where I leeve. My father he is real mad. You guys know who done eet?"

Flaco's face paled suddenly like all his blood had evaporated. "Who me?" he said, voice suddenly high.

"I don't," Keeny said rapidly. "Swear to God, man."

I poked Tran in the ribs, and we both laughed. Anybody could tell they were lying. Tagging had become one of Flaco's new tricks.

"Well, if you know anybody who does that at my place, you tell 'em I'll keeck their butts. You tell 'em?"

"Okay," squeaked Flaco, his voice even higher.

"My brother he's got some spray paint, huh, Flaco?"

"Shut up, Dolores!"

She said, "I'm telling."

Well, Avila's threat calmed down the two warriors, and they started acting pretty much normal. As we rode across town in the bus, Dolores — sitting in front of us — kept turning around and making faces at me. "Hey, I theenk you got another girlfriend, Ryan," Avila teased. "Wait'll I tell Leenda."

It made me proud that he knew Linda liked me, but I sort of shrugged it off. Then Flaco's little sister began gathering spit at the front of her mouth and blowing bubbles like she'd chewed soap. She was real good at it and made some big ones. When Flaco noticed her, he barked, "Stop it, Dolores! That's grossisimo!"

I thought it was pretty neat.

"I'm telling my mother you yelled at me," she threatened.

By the time we arrived at the mall, everybody was talking and laughing like always, and Tran had drawn a small Mickey-Mouse tattoo on Dolores's hand. She giggled and held it up like it was gold or something.

The Plaza was this big, t-shaped building in the middle of a humungous parking lot. The mall was air-conditioned inside, cold like Alaska, and its aisles were wide as streets and lined with all these shops, big and small — pet stores and record stores and sports stores and clothes stores and tobacco stores: everything in the world it seemed like. In the center of it, where all the aisles met, was a fountain, and there were vending stands selling food and flowers and other stuff, and fancy benches to sit on too. I'd only visited it a couple of times with my aunt and uncle, and it seemed terrific to me. Avila and Alphabet had never been there before, so they wandered around open-mouthed, staring at everything. Flaco and Keeny claimed they'd come several times on weekends during that period when I wasn't seeing much of them, and they were acting like guides, showing us these real cool things: they had to start with all the guns in one store, then pro-basketball-team uniforms in another, posters of singers and movie stars in another one.

There weren't that many other kids at The Plaza because the public schools were in session, but we saw these two real pretty ninth-grade cheerleaders from the Catholic high school. I remembered them from the championship game we'd played there.

They ignored us but we sure didn't ignore them. They wore gym shorts and brief t-shirts and more make-up than grown-up women did; their tan legs and bellies looked *excellent.* When they walked, their arms thrust in unison like they were practicing some routine — left ones out, right ones across their chests; then lefts up, rights down. A minute later, both arms were spinning until the right ones were out and the left ones were across their chests, then their rights shot up and their lefts were out; they clapped twice with arms in front of them and each one's left leg kicked back briefly. Whoa! Just the sight of real cheerleaders up close took my breath away.

"How come we stopped," whined Dolores.

"Because," her brother growled.

After the high-school girls wandered away, the two gang guys swaggered a step or two, then Dolores complained, "I gotta go potty."

"Well, go," snapped Flaco.

"My mother said you gotta take me."

"Oh damn!" he said as he walked her to a toilet, then

waited for her. The rest of us were laughing. He sure looked tough standing there outside the girls' restroom.

We kind of split up after that. Keeny led Avila and Alphabet into a sporting goods store, but Dolores wanted to go to a K-Mart that occupied one entire end of the mall, so I walked in with Flaco and her. Once inside, I saw the electronics section across the room — three walls covered with T.V. sets, all of them on at once, each picture with slightly different colors glowing but with no sound.

Flaco stopped. "Hey, you ever been on T.V., Dolores?" he asked, sounding real sure of himself.

"Nuh-unh," she shook her head.

"How 'bout you, man?"

I shook my head.

"I been on real T.V. lots of times," he boasted.

I didn't say anything, but it sounded like a typical Flaco story to me.

Dolores began probing her nose with a finger. "Neally?" she snorted.

"Yeah, neally," he snorted back, imitating her. "Would you stop picking your nose. It looks grossisimo. You wanta be on T.V.?"

She pulled her finger from her nose and examined something on the end of it. "Uh-huh," she nodded quickly.

All of a sudden, the cheerleaders were standing so close to us that I could smell their perfume. One said, "I think Richard's just so foxy" (both hands over heads, right knees lifted).

"Oh, he's got great buns," the other replied, and they giggled (forearms twirled twice across chest).

"And Sandy she told me he likes her" (left arm up, right arm down).

"She's a liar. And besides, she's fat" (right arm thrust forward, left crooked, fist resting on hip).

"Sammy's so fine, and he's quarterback on the junior varsity" (right arm up, left arm down).

Flaco sucked in his breath, pulled back his small shoulders, and tried to look tough. They ignored him. "Are you gonna vomit?" his sister asked him, and I had to laugh.

"Oh, shut up," he said.

"I'm telling my mother."

At the electronics department, a television camera that moved back and forth was set up on a counter, and a big t.v. set near it showed its picture. "Look at that screen," Flaco said, then he stood in front of the camera and flexed his thin arms. "Hulk Hogan," he said, posing like the wrestler, his home-made tattoo clear on the screen.

Dolores squealed, "I could see you! I could see you on T.V."

"Of course you could, man. Didn't I tell you." He scratched under his arm like a monkey, glancing at the screen but he suddenly looked dizzy, and giggled, saying, "Everything's like on the wrong side if I look at the screen man, bass-ackwards."

"I'm not a man," said Dolores. "Could I be on it now? Could I?"

Flaco ignored her because those two cheerleaders were wandering near once more, so he struck his gang-member pose, watching himself grimace on the screen as he bent his arms in front of his chest with first and third fingers extended in what I guess was supposed to be a mob's secret salute. He thought he looked real dangerous I'll bet, but he just looked dopey to me.

Dolores's voice grew higher. "I'm telling my mother."

"Shut up," he snapped.

Flaco hunched his shoulders and began moving like a Soul-Train dancer, one hand still extended in a gang salute, the other pumping.

I was watching him on the screen, laughing because he looked so serious and so goofy at the same time, then I noticed he was moving toward a display of video tapes. He must've seen it too because he sort of dodged, but I

161

guess he was looking at the screen because he sidestepped the wrong way, right into it.

"Watch it!" I called a second before we heard the crash, and on the screen I saw the video display disintegrate and a black-clad clown stumble and fall right into the middle of it.

For a moment everything seemed quiet, then I heard high-pitched giggles — the two cheerleaders were laughing.

Then another image popped onto the T. V. screen: Dolores, too close—her head big, eyes wide, mouth gaping, whole face curving like melting plastic.

"What in the world did you do?" demanded a clerk.

Flaco stammered, "Ah...that little girl she pushed me, man."

"You big fibber!" said his sister. "I'm telling!"

"She didn't touch him," I said.

Far in the background, I could just make out the disappearing forms of two cheer leaders (left arms out, right arms up, knees prancing). On the T.V. screen I saw the brave body of a gang member fallen while defending his turf. He looked at me and crooked his left arm across his chest, then his fingers thrust out in a gang salute.

What a dork.

"You're out of here," the clerk snapped at Flaco..

"When we get home I'm telling my mother on you!" his sister announced.

➤

**Chapter 31**
# "The Inspector"

Flaco was grounded for a little while after that. I only saw him at school, but he kept playing that role, making funny hand signals and acting like he knew some big secret...unless, of course, Avila or Alphabet was around. He was too smart to want to attract too much attention from them or to accidentally make them mad.

To me, though, he was like a little kid saying, "Play like I'm a tough gang banger, okay?" But he still had Keeny following him around like a polliwog's tail, which shows there's always somebody even dumber than a pendejo. The next thing I knew Flaco started carrying cigarettes, then so did Keeny. They coughed and even gagged sometimes when they tried to smoke them, and Flaco asked me only once, "Aren't you gonna try one, man?"

"Heck no."

He didn't start his "chicken" routine because I guess it'd dawned on him that I was getting way too big for him to mess with.

After the big mall adventure though, I had someone following me around. Flaco's little sister Dolores would see me on the playground at Guadalupe, and she'd come over with her friends to say hi. She seemed to think we were big pals since we'd shared Flaco's K-Mart catastrophe, and I did kind of like her. She saw right through her bad-ass brother.

I returned home from school one day, two or three weeks after our visit to Valley Plaza, and I heard my grandmother lecturing into the telephone: "...but I tell you the man has let his yard go to weeds. The entire neighborhood could burn. He is a *terrible* menace." I had just munched a pomegranate at Mr. Samuelian's yard and she eyed the tell-tale red stains around my mouth as she spoke those words.

Once she hung up, Abuelita thrust her chin in my direction. "Now the madman will have to conform — or get out," she asserted. "I have called the Fire Marshal, and he is sending an Inspector." In triumph, she strode from the house to inform Mrs. Alcala.

Just then David Avila arrived with his school books and called, "Hey Ryan, you gonna study?"

"Yeah."

We walked next door, and I was troubled. I didn't know what to tell to Mr. Samuelian.

"Ah," said my neighbor, "this afternoon David will tutor you in Spanish."

"He don' even know how to say pendejo right," Avila said. "Voy a ensenarlo, pendejo."

"Gracias, pendejo," I replied, but my voice was flat.

Avila could tell I was troubled, and he said, "Que paso, Ryan?"

I started to explain, then turned to Mr. Samuelian and said, "Listen, I've gotta tell you what my grandma just said."

I did, and he seemed to think for several moments, then he patted my shoulder, saying, "Thank you for informing me, Manuel. Now don't be concerned. You boys need to study. I'll deal with the inspector if he comes."

The next morning an Inspector did indeed arrive, and I joined my grandmother with most of the other neighbors gathered next to the official white car in front of Mr. Samuelian's yard. Before long, the inspector (stern in a blue uniform and white cap) and our neighbor (pleasant in rumpled khakis) were wandering together through the dense plants. When they neared the front of the yard, I heard the blue-clad man order brusquely, "These'll all have to come down. We don't allow overgrown weeds in Bakersfield."

"But they aren't weeds," responded our neighbor pleasantly.

"What do you mean, these aren't weeds? I can see what they are. Weeds!" snapped the Inspector.

"What is a weed, then?" was Mr. Samuelian's gentle reply.

The uniformed man stopped walking, positioned his hands on his hips, and growled, "You trying to get smart with me?"

"It is a serious question," the old poet assured him. "What is a weed?"

The officer glanced away from our neighbor toward all of us gawking there by the fence, then returned his gaze to Mr. Samuelian, "It's something that grows no matter what, and where you don't want it, and these are weeds."

"But I planted most of them. They all grow where I want them, and I'm pleased with them. How can they be weeds?"

"Because," the blue-clad man explained with tight lips, "a weed is a weed, and those things are all weeds, everything but that rose on the fence there, anyway."

"That is a wild rose. It grows where I don't want it no matter what."

The face above the uniform reddened and seemed to

165

swell like a balloon being blown up. For a moment I thought the Inspector would grab Mr. Samuelian, but instead he jerked a pad from one pocket and began scrawling into it. "You have exactly seven days to cut these weeds," he spat, "or we'll do it for you at your expense. See that it's done!"

Our neighbor simply nodded.

The officer thrust his pad toward Mr. Samuelian, who dutifully signed it, then accepted his copy. The inspector — eyebrows knit in a tight V, the tips of his ears still maroon — spun away and didn't say a word. He plodded to his car, seemed to leap inside, started the engine, then roared away, not looking back.

While that was happening, the old poet did not move. He watched the vehicle trail dust as it disappeared, then glanced at all of us gathered on the dirt between his yard and the street. Finally, he shrugged, put his copy of the ticket in a pocket, and smiled at us. "Would anyone like a plum?" he asked.

Everyone began talking and laughing at once, flooding onto his yard, everyone but my grandmother. I wouldn't have noticed her wandering alone toward our house except that Mr. Samuelian's eyes followed her. "Poor, lonely woman," he said.

➢

166

## Chapter 32
# "The Stroke"

When I returned home after the...what can I call it?...the fiesta in Mr. Samuelian's yard, I couldn't find Abuelita. She wasn't in the kitchen or in the front room watching our little television set. Finally I tapped at her bedroom door, but she didn't answer. Then I checked the bathroom: no luck. I wondered if she'd gone back outside without me noticing, but I couldn't see her anywhere in the yard.

Then, I thought I heard something from her bedroom. I went back to the door and tapped it, listening real close with my ear against the wood. At first I didn't hear anything, then a moan scared me. I pushed open the door and saw my grandma sprawled on the floor. "Abuelita! Abuelita!" I cried, kneeling next to her. "Are you okay?"

She didn't answer, but her eyes were opened and stunned-looking, like somebody'd socked her.

"Let me help you up," I said, but I couldn't because she was so limp, and I wasn't strong enough. Finally, I said, "I'll be right back, Abuelita, honest," and I sprinted out the door and ran to Mr. Samuelian's yard. He was cleaning up after the celebration. I think I was crying because he dropped his rake and met me halfway.

167

"What's wrong, Manuel?" he immediately asked. "What's wrong, my boy?"

"My grandma's on the floor, and she can't get up. Can you help me?"

"On the floor, you say?"

"She's on the floor, and I can't lift her. Please help."

"Of course," he said.

When we got back to the house, Mr. Samuelian knelt next to Abuelita, checked her breathing, took her pulse and spoke soothingly, then he said to me, "You stay with your grandmother." He turned toward Abuelita and explained, "I'm going to call for an ambulance, Mrs. Higuera."

I held my grandmother's hand, and explained over and over again, as much to comfort me as her, that an ambulance was on its way. Her eyes told me she understood, but she did not speak. "Mr. Samuelian's calling right now," I said. "He really is." Her hand felt cool and smooth like glass.

Our neighbor returned saying, "They'll be here soon." Then he spoke to my grandma: "Let me put this pillow under your head. Manuel, put that blanket over your grandmother."

Abuelita stirred, seemed to be trying to say something, then settled once more.

The lady in the ambulance said I couldn't ride along, but Mr. Samuelian told me he'd telephone Jefe, who owned that old truck, and have him drive me to the hospital. "You'd better call your mother, though," he said, "and your uncle."

"Okay," I said, "but first call Jefe. I don't want Abuelita to be alone."

"Of course, my boy." He dialed, spoke briefly, then said, "Jefe will be right over. Now telephone your family, please."

168

I called Uncle Tuti but only got his answering machine. Rats! That meant Mama was the only adult in the family I could reach.

She wasn't home either, so I told Tía Ysabel. She got so upset I wasn't sure she'd remember what I said. Everything seemed to be going real slow, the phone calls, the bell ringing, then the wait for a ride, everything.

Jefe and Ramon finally chugged up in that decrepit pickup that looked like it was one snort away from the junkyard. All four of us piled into the cab and we hurried to Memorial Hospital. As we drove, Jefe said, "Remember the last time we went to the hospital?"

"That old man," he said, pointing a bent brown finger at Jefe, "he tried to wrestle a range cow up at Dick Scaramella's place two, three years ago, and he busted a rib. I had to drive us down here."

"But he don' know how to drive too good," added Jefe, "so I just tol' him what to do and he pointed the truck the right direction. He only hit that one other car — in the parkin' lot there. But he sure scared the tamales out of some people."

Ramon grinned proudly. "Purty good, huh. I didn't want that old man to kick the bucket."

Mr. Samuelian chuckled softly and shook his head, but I could only think of my grandmother. I didn't want *her* to kick the bucket.

At the hospital it was scary. I couldn't see Abuelita and the lady at the front desk didn't act real friendly when she was asking me questions about insurance and who'd be paying, and where my mother "or some responsible party" was, stuff like that. I completely forgot about my Aunt Ysabel, and kept saying my mother would come pretty soon. Just when I was feeling like I might start bawling, Mr. Samuelian eased past me and said pleasantly, "Please page Dr. Minasian. Tell him Sarkis Samuelian wishes to speak with him."

"Well," said the woman, "I..."

"Please," insisted my neighbor.

"Just a moment."

A second later, I heard these gongs echoing through the halls, and it seemed like we waited for a long time again, then there was a buzz and the lady said something into the telephone. "He'll be right here," she announced, eyebrows raised.

Almost immediately a dark, bearded man in a white coat emerged from a door behind us, calling, "Ah, Sarkis, how are you?"

"Fine, fine Arnold. And your mother, is she well?"

"She still bosses me, and I'm forty now with a family of my own," smiled the doctor. He nodded at each of us.

"These are my friends, Arnold, Jefe Lopez and Ramon Contreras, the famous vaqueros. And this young man is Manuel Ryan, my neighbor. His grandmother has just been admitted, and his mother and uncle are out of town, so they can't provide information. Would you be so kind as to inform this nice lady that I'll assume financial responsibility for Mrs. Guadalupe Higuera's treatment."

"No problem," said the bearded man. "Marlene, place my name on the guarantee and see that an adult in the family signs a release as soon as possible."

"Yes, Doctor."

"Where's the patient now?" he asked the lady.

"She's in E. R., Doctor."

"And you, young man, you're worried about your grandmother, aren't you?"

"Yes sir, I sure am," I choked.

"Just a moment. May I use the phone," he asked, and the lady handed it to him. "Thanks."

He punched several buttons and said, "Marge? Arnie Minasian here. Have you got a Guadalupe Higuera there?

She's my patient now, so go ahead and work her up. Is she stable? Okay, I'll be down in a few minutes."

It seemed like it took forever for him to finish, but when he hung up, he smiled and said, "Well, she's resting. Dr. Minkow said it appears she's had a stoke. It doesn't appear to be a life-threatening situation, but we can't be absolutely certain yet. She says your grandmother has asked for a priest, so you should call one. I'm sure his presence will comfort her." He placed a large hand on my shoulder. "I'll take care of her, and I'll let you see her as soon as possible. Nice meeting you gentlemen," he shook hands with Jefe and Ramon, then hugged my neighbor, and hurried up the main hallway.

"He's the God-son of my sister," Mr. Samuelian explained as the doctor departed, then he turned toward that lady and asked, "Where do I sign?"

"That won't be necessary," she said, almost sadly I thought. "Dr. Minasian has assumed full responsibility for the patient."

Late that afternoon, after Momma called to tell me she was on her way, I determined to telephone my father. I couldn't find the name of the town where I'd written it down. Shoot! I rooted around my grandmother's address book, but only found the name of the company, "Cable Exploration," that he had gone to work for when he left. I called the local office and the lady I talked to was real nice, but she didn't know where he was now, or if he was even still on their payroll. That's when I got the idea.

"Could you please give me the number of where the big office is, like where all the bosses work?"

The lady chuckled. "You mean Corporate Headquarters? It's in Houston. I'll give you the number of the personnel office."

She did, and when I dialed I reached another lady. I told her I was looking for my dad, and she said, well...yes, she did have a record for a Patrick Ryan, and, yes, he did still work for the company in Alaska, but she couldn't give me his telephone number or address. Company policy. She'd already told me more than she was supposed to.

That stumped me and I was ready to hang up and go into my room and find my blanket, but I said, "Wait! Can I get you to do me a favor? My grandma's real sick. She's in the hospital. Will you please call my dad and just tell him that, and tell him that Manuel called because we need him at home. Please."

For a second...or several seconds...that lady didn't say anything, then she sighed and it sounded like her voice caught. "Sure," she replied, "I can do that much for you."

When that lady hung up, I just stood there, not knowing what to do. Then I remembered the candles under the sink. I found her biggest one, an Our Lady of Guadalupe in a jar, and I carried it to the shelf. Most of the old ones were burned out, so I wedged the new on in, lit it, an began to pray.

I was still praying when my mom arrived.

## Chapter 33
# "Good Neighbors"

That next afternoon when Mom and me returned from visiting Abuelita at the hospital, Mr. Samuelian and his "one-eyed" brother greeted us. "Mrs. Riley," our neighbor said, we have taken the liberty of preparing a meal for you and Manuel. The tortillas are from Mrs. Alcala, they're delicious. We sampled one...or two," he smiled.

"Oh, thank you Mr. Samuelian," said my mom.

"Do you know Haig, my brother?"

"Manuel has spoken of him, but no, we haven't met."

The larger Samuelian bowed as he said, "My pleasure, Missus."

"Hi," I said.

"You haven't been playing with that slingshot, I hope," said Haig Samuelian. "Remember my eye."

I laughed, but my mother stopped me. "Manuel!" she said. "I'm surprised at you! Don't laugh at the misfortunes of others."

"It's all right, Missus," smiled the larger man, and he rapidly moved the patch from one eye to the other.

"Oh!" Mom said.

I laughed again.

"But why...?" she asked.

"A long story, Missus."

I exchanged glances with the Samuelians, then our neighbor said, "Haig repaired that leak in the roof and we cleared the drainage pipe that troubled la señora. We want things to run smoothly when she returns. Let us know what needs to be done. Will she be home soon?"

"Just a few more days, Dr. Minasian says."

"And have you located your brother Arturo yet?"

"Yes, that darn guy. He and the family were up at Monterey. They're on their way back now, but I really gave him the devil for not telling us they were leaving. He's always been independent like that."

As we spoke, Jefe and Ramon approached, the latter carrying a large jar. "Tenemos un regalo para la senora," he said, and he handed me a container of salsa.

"Gracias," I said.

"O gracias," my mother added. "Won't you all come in and join us, please," she urged. "We can share this wonderful food."

Around the small table, Momma explained that Grandma had indeed suffered a stroke that obscured her peripheral vision on one side, but that it had caused no other long-term damage. "Dr. Minasian thinks that surgery to clear the arteries in her neck will probably be necessary once she's recuperated from this."

"She's a strong woman," Mr. Samuelian said.

"Yes," said his brother, "she reminds me of the woman I freed from kidnappers during the great Fresno uprising."

"Really?" my mother said.

"What a battle!" asserted the "one-eyed" man. "Even today heroic men faint at the memory. But when I was through with the villains, they were subdued...even though one tried to poke my eye out! Their teeth rolled across the street like flung dice," exclaimed the hero.

Mr. Samuelian cut off the story. "We should perhaps

put fresh paint on the doors and whitewash the fence, Haig," he suggested. "What do you think?"

"What? Ah...well, yes. Yes indeed, Sarkis."

"If you do, Manuel and I will certainly help," my mother said. "Let's paint the door and window trim blue. Mama thinks evil spirits can't cross blue borders."

"Is that right?" observed the larger Samuelian.

"Yes, I've read about that," our neighbor nodded.

Haig stood and announced, "I'll go look in the shed to see what colors we've got." Then he left.

Ramon said, "That brother of yours he tells some good ones. He is muy fuerte. No?"

"Fuertísimo," agreed Jefe.

Mr. Samuelian smiled. "Yes, he did indeed fight all those battles, but they have become somewhat more...ah...more, as they fade into memory. I was quite small as a boy, yet no one ever bullied me...not twice, certainly, because they had to deal with Haig."

"Gosh," I said.

"Speaking of battlers, Manuel, how are Tran and David. I haven't seen them for several days."

I grinned. "David's afraid of your brother. Remember how Haig chased him back when David was after me? Anyways, they've been studying at the library."

"Those two, David and Haig, are much alike. But David now has nothing to fear because he is no longer the boy my brother chased. That David was a bully. Is he still doing better in school?"

"He really is. He might even make the honor roll."

"Wonderful! Now that really is muy fuerte."

"Who're you talking about?" asked Momma.

"A kid that used to chase me home and call me names."

Just then I heard a voice bellowing from the yard: "Maaaaan-ny! Maaaaan-ny!"

"That's Flaco," I said.

175

Momma shook her head and smiled. "Doesn't he ever knock?"

"Nope."

"A good boy," said Mr. Samuelian, "but a little reckless."

Haig had just reentered the house and he asked, "Shall I dispatch that young scamp?"

"Can I go out, Mom?"

"If you mean 'May I,' the answer is yes."

Haig Samuelian squared his shoulders and asked, "Have I told you of the time the bruiser Tashjian stood in front of our house and howled my name like that, challenging me to join him in combat? Well,..."

I went out and found Flaco and Keeny, in gang costumes (no cigarettes tucked behind their ears for a change, though) along with Avila and Alphabet. "How's your grandma, man?" Flaco asked.

"She's better," I said. She'll get to come home pretty soon. "Qué pasó, guys?"

"Oh, nothin' special. We just thought you might want to shoot hoops or somethin'," Keeny said.

"Yeah," agreed Tran.

"Sure, but I can't go over to the school right now."

Flaco shrugged. "We could use the old basket there on the tree."

"Yeah," agreed Keeny.

"Okay." I dashed into the house and grabbed my basketball, then dribbled it out onto the dirt, saying, "Let's play H-O-R-S-E."

"Hey Manuel," Flaco called as Tran shot a left-handed hook, "are you married yet?" Same old Flaco.

### Chapter 34
# "Surprises"

Grandma was released from the hospital two days later, and I got to push her in a wheelchair to the car. "The doctor says you're going to be okay, Mama," my mother told Abuelita. "But you have to rest. No more getting yourself in an uproar over little things."

"I have a shadow in my eyes now, m'ija. God has punished me for some terrible sin."

"You've had a little stroke, Mama."

"Who brought me to this hospital?" asked Abuelita.

My mom stopped and said to her mother, "Manuel found you, and Mr. Samuelian took charge and got you taken care of. We owe him a real debt."

"The madman," Abuelita said as though in wonder.

"Anyway, the doctor said it's very important that you stay calm. He also said that if you'd gone in for check-ups the way we asked, you might have avoided this."

Abuelita stared straight ahead. "That shadow is in my eyes," she said, and she fanned the left side of her face with one hand. "God is punishing me."

"Your peripheral vision on the left side has been limited by the stroke, Mama," my mother explained.

We entered Mom's car and she pulled onto the road

toward home. Abuelita still gazed straight ahead. "It is a shadow," she insisted, "a message from God about some evil I have done.

"The shadow is like a ghost, perhaps it is the ghost of someone I have injured. I must examine my conscience and go to Confession."

"It's a stroke, Mama, a physical thing." My mother pulled the car onto the dirt patch in front of our house.

Abuelita gazed at it, then said, "Gracias a Dios."

I thought she was thanking God for being able to return home, but she said to Mom, "Thank you m'ijá for protecting me from evil spirits and more shadows."

"What?" Mom looked surprised, then she smiled. The Samuelians and the old vaqueros had painted our doors and the trim around all of our windows the color of turquoise, so evil spirits couldn't pass through them. My grandma softly beat her breast like she sometimes did when she prayed. "Gracias a Dios," she repeated.

My mother smiled, "Oh, the painting was done by the Samuelian brothers and their friends Jefe and Ramon."

"Those Armenians? Those borrachos?"

As we climbed from the auto, I noticed they had also been at work in our yard. It had been weeded and the dirt had been raked. Our chickens looked confused. Jefe and Ramon, along with the Samuelians, stood next to a pile of weeds and junk on the border of our two yards when we arrived, and they waved to us. Mr. Samuelian had this strange smile on his face.

Mrs. Alcala hurried over as fast as her canes allowed and called, "Ah, Lupe, so good to have you home." She had that same strange smile on her face. Tuxedo followed her like he was happy Abueleta was home, too.

Just then the front door of our house opened, and for a second we all stopped as this tall figure came out and said, "Helen... honey?"

My mother gasped and she choked, "Patrick?"

Daddy didn't wait. He rushed to her and wrapped his arms around her and gave her a great big movie kiss, and I could see that both of them were crying and kissing at the same time. "I've missed you so much, honey," he said. "So much."

They both started to talk at once, but Daddy's voice was louder. "There's something I've gotta say. We're both stubborn, Helen, me most of all. I wanted it my way and you wanted it yours. Well, I don't want to win anymore. I just want to be together."

"Oh, Patrick..." Momma said and they kissed again.

Then he called me, "Manny," and I extended my hand so we could shake, but he swept me off the ground and kissed me. My eyes got all warm. "You're so big," he said.

Abuelita and Mrs. Alcala watched us silently, then my father, not letting go of Momma or me, approached grandma and said, "Mrs. Higuera, I'm real sorry you've been sick. I flew down as soon as I heard." He pecked her cheek and she nodded.

Mr. Samuelian joined us then, with Haig, Ramon and Jefe trailing. "It's good to see you all together again," he grinned, then added, "and may I say that Manuel certainly looks more and more like his father."

That made me proud, but I didn't say anything.

Mom glanced up at Daddy and said, "Patrick, I forgot to call you when Mama got sick. Everything's been so hectic. How did you know?"

"Manny had the company contact me." He turned toward me, and asked, "Why didn't you call me yourself."

"I didn't have your number."

"You had my number, Son," Daddy said. "I sent it the very first time I wrote to you."

"You wrote to me? You never wrote to me, only that Christmas card."

"Sure I did...every week for awhile, but when you didn't answer, I started writing less. I telephoned you too, but your grandmother always said you weren't home."

I remembered some stuff I'd heard and seen, some secret looks and strange hustlings. My eyes settled on Abuelita, who looked at her feet.

I kept remembering more stuff, letters slipped away before I could look at them ("Those are just for me, m'ijito. Do not worry about them."). I didn't want to say anything mean and make my Grandma sicker, but it was like when you look at all the weird stuff in a kaleidoscope, then all of a sudden they form a shape you recognize. I turned to my Grandma and asked, "Do you have my letters, Abuelita?"

She didn't reply.

"Mama?" said my mother.

"Those're mine, Abuelita. I want 'em."

Grandma's mouth moved but nothing came out, and I saw her eyes begin to blink back tears. "I have this shadow now..., " she finally mumbled. "I must light a candle..."

Out neighbors were looking away by then, sort of shuffling back toward their yards.

Rats! I didn't want her to cry, but I wanted my letters, so I said, "It's not fair for you to keep them."

Before I could say more, my father grasped my shoulder and said quietly, "That's enough, son."

Mom turned toward Abuelita, and said, "Let's go inside, Mama. The doctor said you're not supposed to overdo it today. Come on," she urged. "Patrick, you and Manuel come in too, please. I know our neighbors will excuse us."

Once we were inside, Momma said, "You two wait here. I need to talk to my mother," then she and Grandma disappeared into the small bedroom. A minute or two later, my mother and my grandmother returned, and Momma said, "Go on, give them to Manuel. They're his."

My grandmother cleared her throat, then said, "Here m'ijo, these are for you." She held a packet of letters bound by two green rubber bands.

I glanced at Mom and she said, "Take them," so I did. When I worked the rubber bands loose, I saw that the envelopes all open, had all been addressed to me by my father. I showed them to him.

Abuelita didn't face him. Instead she looked down and said to my mother, "I didn't want Manuel to be hurt like you were, m'ija. I was trying to protect him...," she glanced from one to another of us. "Perhaps I was wrong. I have this shadow now because God is punishing me."

"Perhaps you were," Mom said softly. "And perhaps you should have minded your own business. What goes on between Patrick and Manuel and me is private, our business." Her voice began to rise, so she took a deep breath, then said quietly, "I think you owe Patrick and Manuel each an apology."

My father's skin had turned the color of a plum, but he said nothing.

Grandma's own face drooped when she said, "Lo siento mucho, m'ijito" to me.

"Patrick, I am sorry. I didn't mean to...como se dice, mija...," she appealed.

"Meddle?" suggested my mother.

"To meddle. I thought you were gone from us for good."

Daddy's face was still purple, but he managed a tight smile, then said, "It's all right, Mrs. Higuera. We all made mistakes, so there's plenty of blame to go around. I know you didn't mean to hurt Manny. And I never wanted anyone to cry over me either. I love Helen and Manny, and I don't want to be away from them again, ever, even if it means I have to quit my job."

"Really?" asked my mother.

"Really. I'd rather be broke with you than rich without you, honey." They hugged and gave each other another movie kiss, an even longer one.

"You should go where you husband goes, m'ija," my grandmother said, still gazing at the floor.

The words seemed to startle Mom. "What?" she said.

"Your place is with your husband, m'ija."

"Mama, you're the one who insisted that I had to stay close to you!"

"I was wrong about that, too. I just didn't want you to move away forever" — tears came into Abuelita's eyes and her voice choked — "...and leave me alone, but now I know I have good neighbors that will take care of me."

My mother embraced her then and kissed her cheek. "It's okay, Mama."

My dad approached and put his long arms around both of them. "Alaska's just been temporary, Mrs. Higuera. I never intended to stay away permanently or to keep your family away."

"I was afraid of being an old lady alone," Abuelita sobbed lightly. I'd never heard her talk this way before, and my own heart got all heavy. It was so sad, she was I mean, and I was sorry I'd been mad at her before. "I am still afraid, but I do not want to face God with sin in my heart. I have been given this warning...this shadow." She waved one hand next to her face.

I heard a car pull up in front of the house.

"No one's going to leave you alone, Mrs. Higuera. I'm not leaving anyone in my family again."

Just then Uncle Tuti bursts in the front door. "Mama!" he said, "We just got back. How are you?"

"She's fine," said my mother. "We all are."

"Hey, Pat!" he said.

182

## Chapter 35
# "Linda"

I read every single letter my dad had sent me — about fishing for salmon, about his work, about meeting some real Eskimos, about seeing Kodiak bears and killer whales and icebergs, about lots of stuff, but mostly about how he missed Momma and me, how he even dreamed about us. I read some of them twice. I was sure glad he'd come back. Momma was too. I could tell by the way they kept touching each other that next morning and giving movie kisses. When I left for school, my dad walked part way with me and he had one arm around my shoulders, and I didn't even care who saw us. It was totally cool.

When Linda and me strolled home after classes, she was smiling, happy for me. "Your dad came home? That's so neat Manuel. And your grandma's better too?" We were holding hands.

I was thinking that I'd like to give Linda a movie kiss, so I stopped and gazed at her face. It seemed all soft and I thought, Now! Now's the time to kiss her, here in front of the whole world. I sucked in my breath and asked, "Linda, can I kiss you?"

She looked shocked, but smiled and said, "Yes, Manuel."

In the movies, people always close their eyes, so I

moved my face close to hers and felt this electricity on my skin, then closed my eyes and my lips touched her nose. She giggled and I kind of jumped.

"Manuel," she said, and her face moved toward mine, and our lips touched, and I felt like I'd never have to breath again. Boy, my trousers got real tight, but my heart got even tighter.

Just then I heard, "Two little lovebirds sittin' in a tree, K-I-S-S-I-N-G!" I turned to see Flaco and Keeny.

"Hey, Keeny," said Flaco real loud, "I told you Manuel *liiiiikes* her."

I started to automatically deny it, the words almost came out, but instead I said, "You darn right I do! What do you want to do about it?"

"Do too!" he snapped. Then he blinked, maybe realizing what he'd just said.

"What do you two want to do about it?" I repeated.

They blinked, looking like my grandma's chickens, then Flaco shrugged, "Nothin', I guess." He said to Keeny, "Come on, let's go. Manuel's no fun."

As they departed, Linda squeezed my hand and smiled at me, her eyes twinkling, and she quickly kissed me on the mouth once more.

When I finally got back to my house that afternoon, I wanted to tell my father what had happened, but knew it was something private between Linda and me. I could hardly think of anything but kissing her again.

Daddy was next door helping our neighbor and his brother trim the last of his weeds. It made me sad to see them do that, and I said so. "Never mind, Manuel," Mr. Samuelian assured me, "we're not killing them. These will grow back. They will last longer than that inspector's memory. Life is a cycle, so they aren't going to be lost."

"In some ways, life is a *bicycle*," Haig Samuelian pronounced.

"A bicycle?" I said,

"A bicycle," said Haig. "When things go too easily, we can slide like a bike on ice, taking too much for granted. A few rough spots provide traction."

My dad said, "Well, we ought to have pretty good traction for our family by now. I'm ready for us to slide a little."

"A little sliding is good," agreed Haig.

"Yes," added Mr. Samuelian, "if you expect life to be difficult, you will not be disappointed, and life's little joys will not be taken for granted.

"A mi es lo mismo," I said.

My father's eyes blinked at me. "Manny," he said, "you're talking Spanish."

"I'm taking it at school, dad."

Mr. Samuelian smiled: "He's also taking it in the neighborhood."

"And a good thing, too," said my dad. "I've learned that nowadays you'd better be a least bilingual."

For some reason, that reminded me. "Hey, Dad," I said as I reached into my book bag, "Mr. Mancuso, my teacher, he made me bring this thing home again and gave me this new one to fill out." I handed him the old copy of that form about ethnic background, plus the fresh one.

"Pacific Islander?" he said, smiling at me. "What is this?"

"It's this form everybody in the class has to fill out, but I'm not on there."

"Hmmm. Listen to this," my dad said to the other men. "White/Euro-America, Native American, Asian, Black/ Afro-American, Middle-Eastern, Pacific Islander, Mexican/Chicano, Other Hispanic."

"And you checked what?" our neighbor asked.

"Well, the first time, Abuelita had me cross off the 'Other' in 'Other Hispanic,' but the teacher gave it back to me, so I marked 'Chicano' the next time, and he sent it home again, so I just marked 'Pacific Islander' because I thought the whole thing was dumb."

"It is," agreed my father. "You could just as well mark all of them."

"I understand the rationale for such a survey, but these old, narrow terms make no sense," Mr. Samuelian said. "They confuse racial and geographical and cultural categories. Some body needs to take a look at real Americans, not merely at traditional words. We are a blended people, culturally and physically. With your permission, Pat, may I make a small addition?"

"To the form?" said my father. "Sure Sarkis. Why not?" and he handed it to our neighbor.

Mr. Samuelian withdrew a ball-point pen from his breast pocket, then drew a small square below the others on the list and wrote next to it "AMERICAN."

He handed the sheet back to my father and said, "May I suggest that you check that new box for Manuel. Tolerance is our virtue, variety is our uniqueness, and braiding differences is our strength."

Daddy glanced at it for a long moment, like he was thinking about what Mr. Samuelian had just told him, then smiled. "If I can borrow your pen, Sarkis," he said. "I'll just do that." He checked the new box, then signed the form. "I'll deliver this in to school tomorrow, Manny. "

"Thanks, Dad," I said, real proud he was my father.

"That's the box all of us should check," smiled Mr. Samuelian. "It's too easy to find ways to separate people when what we really need to do is learn to live together."

"Amen," my father said.

"I think Flaco needs a different box," I grinned.

Mr. Samuelian glanced at me for a second, then he said, "None of that pendejo business."

I had to laugh. He was pretty smart for an old guy.

➤

## Chapter 36
# "A Surprise"

I guess I got to thinking that everything would always be fun like the day my Dad came home — you know, like the happy ending of a movie. Even though I had been mad at Abuelita for not giving me my letters, I felt so good about everything else, including that she was home from the hospital, that I just sort of cruised for awhile. Linda and me we started kissing a lot, though not out in the open very much like that first time.

My dad flew back to Alaska, then he returned with the truck and his stuff — including some really neat souvenirs for all of us. Mom went back to L.A. but for just a few days — Uncle Tuti he hired this lady to stay with Grandma and me when Mom was gone — then my mother was back too with all her stuff. She and my dad had to rent a big locker because there wasn't any space at Abuelita's little house for much of it. Grandma got stronger and pretty soon she was walking around with this aluminum walker thing, out in the yard talking to Mrs. Alcala and even to Mr. Samuelian.

In fact, on the second day after she was on her feet, she came outside with me and, instead of turning toward Mrs. Alcala's house, she moved toward Mr. Samuelian's.

"I want to give these tortillas I have made to our neighbor," she said, and I had to blink. I never thought I'd hear that.

When we got to his yard, she handed our neighbor the tortillas and said, "I want to thank you and your brother for all the work you did to help me."

"That's what neighbors are for, Mrs. Higuera," smiled the old poet. "We're all so happy that you're better."

His larger brother, still visiting, bowed as he said, "It was our honor, Missus."

"And I am sorry about that ... ah ... that problem with the inspector," she added.

"No harm done," said our neighbor. "We're delighted that you're home." He extended his hand and at first she looked at it like she didn't know what he was doing, then she smiled, and they shook hands like Avila and Tran making up.

After that they were friends. Not big pals or anything, but friends; Grandma didn't call him "madman" or "dangerous" anymore, and she didn't mind when Alphabet and David and me hung around his yard.

We didn't see as much of Flaco and Keeny as before. They were getting deeper into their gangster game, I guess. Anyways, they sure didn't come around my house very often.

Once both my folks returned, I could tell almost right away things were going to be more like normal than a happy movie. My mom said we had to stay with Grandma because she was sick, although Uncle Tuti had already found us a neat place to rent, and he'd even said he'd even keep paying for that lady to stay with Abuelita. My dad really wanted us to be in a house of our own. He said we needed our privacy, and Mom agreed, but she added, "We can't leave Mama alone right now, I can't. She's just too frail to care for herself."

"Why can't we live in a place of our own, and you can

come over every day? Your brother will pay that woman to..."

"It's not the same, Pat. I'll call Social Services, though, and see what I can find out about help for senior citizens."

He gave in, but I could tell he wasn't real happy.

They had lots more talks about it, taking rides or walks so they could speak privately. And a few times they went away for weekends, while that lady came and stayed with Abuelita and me. I was sleeping on the couch in the little living room then, and my folks were using the bed that had been mine. My grandma was sleeping in her own bed. The house was real crowded, all right, but pretty soon my dad had talked to Abuelita and to Uncle Tuti and to Mom, and they all agree to at least let him build a new bedroom and bath on the back of the house.

That made my dad happy. He'd found a job, too, in the oilfields north of town, not as good as the one in Alaska, but at least he was working and we could all be together.

For a long time I'd been seeing all these dark guys in funny old clothes standing around on mornings in front of the gas station across the street from Guadalupe School. My dad hired two of them to help him build that bedroom, and they went right to work, digging a foundation, pouring cement, then beginning to erect walls. In fact, they did a lot more of the work than he did.

Javier and Angel were their names, and they were from way down in Mexico. They looked like the Aztec faces on the calendar hanging in our kitchen. When they talked to each other it wasn't in Spanish, and one day, wanting to know what language they spoke, I asked, "¿Qué lengua hablan ustedes?

Angel, who was about my size, but a full-grown man and real strong, he said, "La lengua de nuestro pueblo."

The language of their people...or maybe of their village, I wasn't sure which he meant. That didn't tell me much.

189

Javier squinted at me then, and asked, "¿De donde es?"

Where was I from? That seemed like a dumb question. "Who, me? De aquí, por supuesto, Bakersfield."

The two Mexican men grinned at one another, and Javier asked me, "¿Pues, por qué hablas español? ¿Tú eres un norteamericano, no?"

Why did I speak Spanish? It was my turn to laugh. That reminded me of what Flaco and Keeny had once said to me, so I said, "Porque es la lengue de mí pueblo."

They both laughed and so did I. We were pals after that, and I started helping them when I got home from school.

They'd torn a big hole in the wall of what used to be my bedroom and covered it with plastic sheets. Then they finished the new walls and put in windows.

Momma, meanwhile, decided not to look for a job at all for awhile. She would stay home so she could take Abuelita to the doctor and to church and stuff. I didn't mind it being so crowded in the house, as long as we were together.

I guess my folks found some privacy, though, because one afternoon I came home from Linda's, still buzzing from our kisses and touches, and Mom said, "Manuel, I've got some good news for you."

I thought maybe she'd say we could finally buy a computer. "What?"

"You're going to have a little brother or sister."

Wow! Was I ever shocked. At first I couldn't even say anything because I knew right away what my folks had to have done — Father Mario called it "the marriage act." It was the same thing I was thinking about doing with Linda, but it didn't seem right for them, grown-ups and all, married or not. It seemed real nasty. "Oh," I kind of choked, "that's good."

190

"You don't seem too happy," Mom grinned. She looked real pleased about having another baby.

I was thinking that all my friends would know what my mother had let my father do to her. On the other hand, Flaco's Mom was always pregnant, and so was Gary Benevidez's and Anthony Martinez's. Mrs. Lawrence down the street, too. But I didn't care about them. Rats! These were my own folks, and they were wrecking everything by what they'd done. I sure didn't want Linda to know that my own folks were having sex.

I walked next door right away, and when I told Mr. Samuelian why I was upset, he did something he'd never done before: he laughed at me and shook his head. "Manuel, Manuel," he said, "relax. Don't be so self-centered."

"What do you mean, 'self-centered'?"

"You're only thinking of your own comfort or discomfort. How about your parents' feelings?"

That wasn't what I was talking about, so I said, "Oh yeah, why did they have to go and do...do *that*... then get pregnant and all?"

He stopped grinning. "Oh," he said, "now I see more clearly what's troubling you. I thought maybe you were jealous of the new baby. Let's start again. Sit down. I don't want to be too explicit, but you're a young man now, not a child, and you should understand that sex is natural and frequent in a loving relationship. It is not exceptional. Your parents love one another, and they have simply chosen to have another baby. Aren't you glad they're back together?"

"Sure." I replied, but I was thinking of what he'd said: sex is natural and frequent in a loving relationship. Wow! I sure didn't know that, and wasn't even sure I believed it. At school, Father Mario made it sound unnatural and infrequent in any relationship. "You mean grown-ups do it a lot?"

191

"As I said, it is not an infrequent way for married people to express their love for one another. You should be happy that your parents love one another. Some of your friends aren't that lucky."

Some sure weren't. Some didn't even have parents at all... that I knew of, anyway. Well, I decided to think over what he'd said. Besides, it might be fun to have a little brother or sister, as long as no one teased me.

## Chapter 37
# "Dark Days"

So much was happening so fast in my life that I felt out of breath a lot of the time. Mostly when I was with Linda. I wanted to kiss her all the time, and touch her in places where Father Mario said it was a sin. And I could tell she wanted me to, even if she wouldn't let me.

I tried to tell her what was going on in me, but it was real difficult to talk about. I was walking her to and from school every day, and sometimes if her folks weren't home, I'd go in and we'd turn on the TV, then not watch it, just smooch and stuff on the couch. Sometimes my privates would hurt so much afterwards that I could hardly walk home.

Then one morning, as I was on my way to Linda's house so I could walk her to school, David Avila shouted to me from down the block. "Ryan! Hey Manuel!"

"Hey, Avila," I called back, waving at him.

He jogged up to me, and asked, "Did you hear about Keeny?" His face looked grim, like he was going to punch somebody.

"Keeny? No. What'd he do, get in trouble?"

"He got shot last night. Eet was on the news. Heem and Flaco was een front of that pool hall, the Eight-Ball, all dressed een those pendejo outfeets, and somebody drove by and shot Keeny."

I couldn't say anything. I didn't have words for this, or even ideas. Finally, I choked, "No lie?"

"De veras."

We stood there looking at one another. "Is he okay?"

"The news guy he said he's hurt bad een the hospital."

"He's not dead?"

"No."

Flaco wasn't at school that day, so I couldn't ask him what happened, but I heard all kinds of stories. Fat Anthony he said this guy told him that Flaco and Keeny went to the Eight-Ball to buy some cucarachas, marijuana cigarettes. Gary Benevidez said he'd heard that Flaco'd had a gun himself, one he got from his cousin in L.A., and he'd started a gunfight with some bad guys. That sounded like a story Flaco'd make up. Carmen she said her cousin from la Loma told her some guys from a gang over there shot at Keeny after Flaco and him made a different gang's sign at them. Luther Dupree, whose mother worked at Mercy Hospital, he said that Keeny was paralyzed and couldn't even walk or anything, but that Flaco didn't get hit. The shooting was all anyone talked about.

There was a special assembly at school that afternoon. Father Mario announced that Keeny had been injured, and gave us this long lecture about gangs and weapons and responsibility. He sounded real mad. He said that Keeny was in "intensive care" and that he couldn't have visitors, but that we should pray for him. He led us all in the rosary, and I knelt there and prayed as hard as I could for Keeny. I didn't notice the kind of screwing around that usually occurred when we were supposed to say the rosary, except that dumb Terry Dominguez cut a loud one and giggled, so Avila poked him in the ribs so hard he almost keeled over. That was the end of that.

When I walked Linda home that afternoon, she asked,

"Manuel, did you ever think about dying? What it's like, I mean?"

"One time after my cat died when I was little," I said, "I woke up at night and I was alone and real scared, and I thought that must be it, quiet and dark and scary, and I cried for Tiger Tom. My mom said it's not like that when you die. She said it's like going home."

Linda listened thoughtfully, then asked, "How does she know?"

"I don't know. I guess she just believes. Maybe it's in the Bible or something."

"Do you believe in Heaven and Hell?"

"I don't think so. I just don't know."

"I don't think anybody knows," she said. "I think they just hope stuff."

We were holding hands and kind of strolling. I stopped, and said, "Why not? I mean, if we don't know, why not hope?"

She gazed at me again, like she was thinking, then shrugged, "Why not?"

"I sure hope Keeny doesn't die."

When I arrived home that afternoon, my mother told me that Mrs. Alcala had told her the doctors didn't expect Keeny to ever walk again.

That wasn't fair, and I told her so. She hugged me, but I didn't feel much better. Sometimes I wished I was still little. I looked for my old piece of blanket, but couldn't find it.

When my grandma lit a candle for Keeny, I walked into the other room. God wasn't being fair.

That next morning, I found Mr. Samuelian working in his garden. When he noticed me, he straightened up and asked, "How are you doing, Manuel? Are you looking forward to the new baby?"

"Me, I'm okay, but Keeny's not."

"I know.

I shook my head, "I don't even know for sure what happened to him. There's all these stories at school."

"Yes, I imagine there are," he said, and he put a hand on one of my shoulders. "Mrs. Alcala said Keeny and Flaco had gone down to the Eight-Ball just to hang around the older boys. She said Keeny's mother had warned him not to go there, but he went anyway. They were standing on the edge of a group of older boys when a car drove by, and someone in it shot, and Keeny was hit. That's what they told the police, and that's all the family knows."

He hadn't told me anything I hadn't heard versions of, so I asked, "Is Keeny paralyzed?"

"Yes, he is now. We're all praying for his recovery."

I didn't tell him that I'd decided to stop praying because God wasn't being fair. Instead, I asked, "How come kids like Keeny have to get shot?"

He stopped the way he usually did when he had something serious to say. "They don't have to, my boy, but this one did. He was in the wrong place at the wrong time. I don't think there's any grand scheme involved."

"Megan Estrada, she said God's punishing Keeny."

My neighbor shook his head slowly. "Megan is wrong. It's all a great mystery, but I don't think God works that way. If He did, Keeny wouldn't be high on the list of people to punish. No, God gave us brains, and now He lets us make our own mistakes...like Keeny following Flaco to that pool hall. It was his mistake, not God's."

"It's not fair."

"No," he agreed, "it's not. But it's real. 'Fair' is just a concept. Remember when I told you that for most people life was hard?"

"It's still not fair," I said, then I walked home. Flaco was the one that should have been shot, not Keeny.

➤

196

Chapter 38
# "Visiting Hours"

Flaco didn't come back to school. I wanted him to
so I could beat him up. Us guys heard that his folks had
sent him out of town so the guys that shot Keeny wouldn't
find him. But Carmen said the cops had locked Flaco up
in this prison for kids. Fat Anthony he said Flaco was really dead but nobody would tell. Another guy said that
Flaco had joined the Gavilanes gang and that he had a
machine gun. Despite all the crazy stories at Guadalupe
School — stories that didn't agree very much — the police still hadn't arrested anyone.

We got reports on Keeny every morning at school from
Father Mario. The class — all except me — prayed for
him every day, too. We even lit candles for him, and this
one nun, Sister Immaculata, she started a Novena.

But I wouldn't do any of it because God hadn't been fair.
It should have been Flaco in the hospital.

I hated him.

A couple of weeks after the shooting, Father Mario
announced that Keeny was no longer in "intensive care."
The priest asked all the members of the seventh-grade
basketball team to meet with him that day after school in
the classroom. We assembled — all except Flaco, that is

— and the priest said, "We have been invited to visit Joaquin. Each of you take these notes home to your families, and I'll drive us over in the school van. I want you to meet me in front of school by 6:30. Visiting hours begin at 7:00 p.m. I'll drive you home by 8:30 at the latest."

Linda was waiting to walk with me when the meeting was over, and she got as excited as me when I told her the team would visit Keeny. I was scared too, though —scared of what I'd see. I didn't tell her that. She said for me to be sure to say hi to Keeny from her, and that she'd been praying for his recovery too. We held hands real tight.

Me, I just wondered how Keeny'd look. You know, if he'd have holes in him like guys in comic books sometimes did. I wondered if he'd be real faint like in some movies where guys just kind of gasped words when they tried to talk, stuff like that. Phuc Nguyen, this kid on the team, he claimed he'd seen some shot people when he was little, and they didn't look like the movies; they looked like a butchershop, all meat and blood. I hated for him to tell me that, but I still didn't know for sure what to expect. And I was still mad. I wanted Flaco to have been shot, not Keeny.

When Father Mario ushered us into the hospital, that night, a nurse she told us not to act rowdy or silly. She said Keeny got tired real easy, so be careful.

I couldn't keep myself from feeling uncomfortable ... especially after we filed into his room and actually saw him. Keeny seemed the same except that he had this metal thing around his head that they called a halo, but it looked more like the crown of thorns you see in the old-time pictures of Jesus. And he was skinnier and real pale. Off to his side on this table, somebody had set up a crucifix, and a candle in a little blue jar was burning in front of it.

All the guys on the team got quiet, holding their breaths or something. I didn't mean to, but I said a prayer under my breath: "God, please, please help Keeny. Please."

"Hi," Keeny said, sounding about normal.

We all mumbled hi.

"Hey, Alphabet," he said, "I need you to come in and help me with math. Mr. Mancuso's gonna send my homework to the hospital."

Tran said, "Okay."

"How long do you gotta stay in here, ese?" Gary Benevidez asked.

"I don't know. Till my legs come back, I think. They feel like they're asleep right now. Look, you guys, I can move my arms," and he did, but his hands were all stiff-looking.

I wanted to cry or beat somebody up or something, him having to get excited about just barely moving his arms. I hated it. One of my own hands slid to a pocket where I had hid that little shred of my old blanket I'd finally found. I needed to say something to Keeny, but didn't know what.

For what seemed like a long time everybody was quiet, then Keeny's eyes met mine, and I knew I had to talk. "Good," I finally managed, "now you can practice your free throws."

Father Mario snapped his eyes toward me like I'd cussed or something, but Keeny just laughed and said, "Hey, Ryan, I'll beat you at 'horse' soon as I get out."

"Anybody can beat Ryan," Luther Dupree said, and everyone laughed again, real tight and nervous.

Just then the door wedged open — there wasn't much space left in the room — and in walked Flaco's mother towing her son behind her. Mrs. Rójas had this dark shawl on like she wore to Mass, and Flaco was dressed in regular clothes not all that baggy black stuff. He looked real little. I got mad soon as I saw him, and I wished he'd been shot.

"Mrs. Rójas," nodded Father Mario. "Flaco."

Mrs. Rójas sort of pushed Flaco toward the bed where Keeny laid. Her son kept his eyes down, not looking at any of us. We opened a lane for them. "My son has something to say," she announced.

Flaco's eyes were blinking, and he was still looking down, then he mumbled something.

"Louder!" ordered his mother, her voice cracking like a dry stick.

"Keeny ...," he cleared his throat. "Keeny," he said again, then had to clear his throat once more ..., "I just wanta say ... ah ... I'm like real, real sorry man, ... for ... ah ... what ... happened. I never wanted nobody to get hurt ... exspecially you ...." He looked up then and, I guess, actually saw Keeny. Suddenly Flaco was sobbing just like a little kid right in front of all of us, and I didn't want to beat him up anymore. I didn't want either one of my friends hurt.

Flaco was sobbing when he said, "I ... I ... I'm sorry you got shot ...," he choked on that last word.

Keeny turned his head slightly in that halo thing, moved one of his stiff hands so that it almost touched Flaco, and he said, "Hey, you never done it, ese. Some dumb pendejo did." Then he let out a little chuckle.

One of the guys chuckled too, then others did, and so did I.

So did Flaco, his face wet with tears.

All of us laughed louder, then louder still until tears flowed, and I had to keep laughing so no one would know I was crying. Everybody was laughing and had tears running down their faces.

There wasn't anything else we *could* do.

## Spanish-English Glossary

**A mi es** — To me it is...
**A mi es lo mismo** — To me, it is the same.
**A mi es muy a dificil** — To me, it is very difficult.
**abuela** — grandmother
**abuelita** — literally "little Grandmother"
**abuelo** — grandfather
**ahora** — now
**al contrario, a mí es muy difícil** — to the contrary, for me it is very difficult.
**algunas maneras** — some way; (in) some manner; the opposite of "no way"
**aquí** — here
**bandido(s)** — bandit(s)
**barrio** — neighborhood
**bisabuelo** — great-grandfather
**boca grande** — big mouth
**borracho(s)** — drunk(s)
**bruja/o** — (female/male) witch
**buenas días** — good day; good morning
**burrito** — A tortilla wrapped around beans or other stuffing.
**caballero(s)** — horsemen; gentlemen
**cabrón** — male goat; cuckold ( used as a cuss-word)
**candela** — candle
**carnal** — carnal, flesh; used to mean something like "blood brother"
**chicharron(es)** —fried pork rind(s)
**cholo(s)** — migrants from Mexico
**chones** — underpants
**chorizo** —sausage; slang for penis
**chor'o** — contraction of choriso
**¿cómo estás?, cómo está** — "How are you?"

201

**¿Cómo está mí hermana? ¿Y tu empleo?** — How's my sister? And your job?

**cómo se dice ...** — How do you say it ... ?

**cómo se llama(s)** — literally, "How is it ( How are they) called?"; used like "What's your name?"

**cómo un cholo** — "like a cholo"

**compañero(s)** — pal(s)

**cucaracha(s)** — literally cockroache(s); slang for marijuana cigarette(s)

**curandera** — healer

**curandera (not a) bruja** — healer not a witch

**De aquí, por supuesto** — from here, of course.

**¿De donde es?** — Where are you from?

**de veras** — truly

**¿De veras?** — True?

**difícil** — difficult

**en el inglés** — in English

**enchirito** — a Taco Bell favorite food

**es** — it is

**Es fácil** — it's easy

**¿Es Mamacita?** — Is it mama?

**ese** — used like "guy, dude, or man"

**Ése no le debe ni los buenas días a los Españoles!** — literally, "That one doesn't owe even a good day to the Spaniards."; colloquial meaning, "He isn't even part Spanish.

**fajita** — a popular dish

**fácil** — easy

**familia** — family

**fiesta** — party

**fuerte** — strong

**Fuertísimo** — very forceful; very strong

**gabacho** — negative term for an Anglo-American

**gallinas** — chicken

**gato** — cat

**Gavilanes** — a gang name
**gordo** — fat
**gracias** — thanks
**Gracias a Dios** — thank God
**gringo** — negative term for an Anglo-American
**hasta la vista** — "Until I see you"; a way of saying
    goodbye
**¿Hay problemas?** — Are there problems?
**hijo** — son
**¡Hijole!** — an interjection used like "Wow!"
**Hola** — "hello" or "hi"
**hombre** — man
**indio** — Indian
**inglés** — English
**La lengua de nuestro pueblo** — The language of our
    people ( or village)
**la Llorona** — The Weeping woman, a figure in Mexi-
    can lore
**la loma** — the hill
**la señora** — the lady
**linda** — pretty ("Leenda" is David's pronunciation.)
**Lo siento mucho** — I'm very sorry
**loco** — crazy
**los chisos** — the ghosts; evil spirits
**los otros** — the others ( those different from us);
    outsiders
**los ricos** — the rich [people]
**¡Madre de Dios!** — Mother of God
**mal de ojo** — evil eye
**(el) malcriado(s)** — (the) brat(s)
**Mamacita** — literally, " little mother"; an affectionae
    term
**más** — more
**mayordomo** — boss, foreman
**m'ija** — contraction of "mi hija" meaning " my daugh-

ter"
**m'ijita** or **mi'jita**—contraction for "my little daughter"
**m'ijo** — contraction of "mi hijo," meaning " my son"
**m'ijito** or **mi'jito** — contraction of "mi hijito," literally
" my little son" an (affectionate term)
**mijito** — same as above
**míra — look**
**míre , ¡Míre!** — a command from the verb mirar, " to
look"
**mucho** — much, a lot
**muy** — very
**muy distincto** — very different
**muy fuerte** —very forceful; very strong
**muy hombre** — very manly
**muy indio** — very Indian
**muy lunatica** — literally, very moonstruck; really crazy
**muy peligroso** — very dangerous
**niño(s)** — child(ren)
**no hay** — no there aren't
**no maneras** — no way
**Norteño(s)** — Literaly, a northerner; used to designate
gangs identified with American-born members
**novia** — fiance
**O gracias —** Oh, thank you.
**O, pobrecita —** Oh, the poor little one
**peligroso** — dangerous
**pendeja** — see pendejo — femine
**pendejo(s)** — literally, pubic hair; slang word for
"jerk," etc.
**pirata** — pirate; slang for any person wearing an eye
patch
**pobrecita** — poor little thing
**poco lunatica** — a little crazy
**por favor** — please

**Porque es ...** — Because it is ...

**Porque es la lengue de mí pueblo.** — Because it is the language of my people (my village).

**¿Pues, por qué hablas español?** — Well, why do you speak Spanish?

**Qué lástima** — What a pity.

**Qué lengua hablan ustedes?** —

**¿Qué pasó?** — literally, " What happened?"; also used as a greeting, "What's happening?"

**¿Qué tal?** — a greeting, "How are things?"

**¿Quién es?** — Who is it?

**raton** — rat

**reata** — a rope used by vaqueros, often made of braided leather.

**simón** — yeah

**sombrero(s)** — hat(s)

**Su hermano es muy caballero.** — literally, "Your brother is very [much a] horseman"; colloquial mening, " Your brother is a real man."

**su Mamacita** — Your little mama, an affectionate term.

**su novia** — your fiance

**Sureños** — The s A street gang, tSoutherners.

**"Tenemos un regalo para la senora"** — We have a gift for the lady.

**tía** — aunt

**tío** — uncle

**¿Tú eres un norte americano, no?** — You are a North American, aren't you?

**Tú hablas español tan peor** qué **yo hablo el inglés, pendejo** — "You speak Spanish worse than I speak English, jerk."

**Tú mamá** — Your mama

**un vaquero** qué **rodea el ganado** — literally, " a cowboy who rounds up livestock"; a horse wrangler

**vaquero(s)** — cowboy(s)

**vato** — guy

**¡Ven!** — come

**¡Ven aquí!** — come here

**verdad** — True, truth

**voy a ensárlo** — I'm going to teach it.

**Voy a ensenárlo** — I'm going to teach him.

**Voy a pagárlo en la misma moneda** — literally, "I'm going to pay him with the same money"; colloquial meanng, " I'm going to get even with him."

**¿Y su empleo? ¿Y tu empleo?** — And your job?

**Ya lo hablas mejor qué ...** — "You already speak it better than ..."

**Ya lo hablas mejor qué Manuel** — You already speak better than Manuel does.